The
DARKEST
PRINCE

JILLIAN FROST

The
DARKEST
PRINCE

JILLIAN FROST

For the kinky girls who dream of being stalked and tied up by their book boyfriend.

Taste me, you will see
More is all you need
Dedicated to
How I'm killing you

Metallica, "Master of Puppets"

Also by Jillian Frost

Princes of Devil's Creek

Cruel Princes

Vicious Queen

Savage Knights

Battle King

Boardwalk Mafia

Boardwalk Kings

Boardwalk Queen

Boardwalk Reign

Devil's Creek Standalone Novels

The Darkest Prince

Wicked Union

For a complete list of books, visit JillianFrost.com.

The DARKEST PRINCE

JILLIAN FROST

Chapter One

I LOVE THE SOUND FLESH MAKES WHEN MY KNIFE SLASHES
through it. And as the life drains from a living being, I savor
the moment it takes its final breaths.

Thump.

Thump.

Thump.

Sitting in the grass, with the perfect view of the bay, I filet
the fish squirming in my hand. Its eyes widen, struggling to
survive, desperate for another second of life.

People make the same faces when they're about to die.
Some even beg for their lives. But once my mind is made up,
there's no turning back.

As long as the pain disappears afterward, I don't care who
I hurt. At least I didn't until my adoptive father discovered my
secret that only Bastian knew.

Arlo Salvatore adopted us when we were kids after our
parents were killed in a fatal plane crash. He helped curb my
urges and showed me how not to get caught. My kills have a
purpose.

I hear footsteps behind me. And before he sits beside me, I
know it's Bastian.

My best friend.

My adoptive brother.

Bash is only three months older than me. We've been best

friends since birth, and after tragedy ruined our lives, we became different people. Now, we share the same last name.

We have a family again.

Bastian puts his hand on my thigh, and I try to ignore the tingling sensation that spreads up my leg, hardening my cock. I like how he makes me feel.

Excited.

Turned on.

Scared.

Alive.

"You're making a mess." Bastian digs his fingers deeper into my skin until I snap my head at him. "Damian, what are you doing?"

What am I doing?

Losing my fucking mind.

Trying not to feel everything.

For you.

Bastian keeps me grounded. He's the only person, besides our adoptive father, who can snap me out of my bloodlust.

I *need* him.

Want him.

Crave him.

"I was bored." I drop the fish and the hunting knife on the ground and shrug. "Just killing time before we meet Carl Wellington's granddaughter."

Bastian takes my hands between his and wipes the blood from my skin with the towel. "This has to stop. You promised to chill out with this shit."

His gray eyes meet mine, and I consider touching him. Pressing my lips to his.

He won't let me kiss him.

Not on the lips.

I know this.

But I want to.

Bastian only lets me indulge my fantasies whenever I can't control myself, consumed by bloodlust, needing to kill again.

Before he cleans off the last of the blood, I raise his hand to my mouth and suck his finger, licking it clean. His chest rises and falls faster, his eyes fixed on me.

I know he likes it.

He wants it.

But he hates himself for having feelings for a man. He's been brainwashed to feel shame every time.

We're not gay. I've never looked at another man and felt attraction. Desire. Bash is my exception, and I'm his.

"D," he groans and yanks his finger out of my mouth, wiping his hand on the towel. "Tonight is a big deal for Dad. You have to keep your shit together. We won't get into The Founders Society without Alexandrea Wellington."

Technically, we don't need to marry anyone. We were born into powerful, connected families. Before we became Salvatores, we could gain admittance into any exclusive club in the country.

Bastian Kincaid.

Damian Townsend.

Our former last names guaranteed us a spot with the Founders. But the Salvatores are not from the United States and don't have the same lineage as us.

"I'll be on my best behavior," I tell him. "What do you think I was doing out here?" I roll my shoulders. "Just blowing off some steam."

His thumb traces his bottom lip, and my eyes follow the simple movement.

I lick my lips.

He stares at mine.

"We can't do that anymore," he whispers.

"No," I fire back. "You don't have to be embarrassed by me."

"I'm not." He shoves his fingers through his dark caramel hair, brushing it off his forehead. "Fuck. It's not like that. You know I love you."

"As a friend," I toss back at him. "A brother?"

He swallows hard. "Yeah."

I understand obsession.

But love?

Not so much.

I don't know how it feels to love someone. What I feel for Bastian goes beyond love.

I want to possess him, crawl so far beneath his skin I become one with him. If I believed in soulmates, he would be mine. The one person I can't live without. He's like a drug to me. An addiction. And after he let me get high on him once, I couldn't stop.

I *can't* quit him.

I tug at the grass with my fingers, needing to keep my idle hands occupied. Anything to stop myself from thinking too much about what I can't have. Whenever I need to think, I come out back, sit on the lawn, and stare at the bay.

The waves crash on the beach below us. And with the drop being at least a hundred feet, I love being inches from the cliff's edge, knowing at any second, it could all end.

I'm not afraid to die.

I only fear one thing—losing Bastian. He's my reason for living on the worst days. When we're together, it gives me hope. And sometimes, that's all I have.

Hope for more.

More of him.

Bash must notice I'm getting antsy because he gets on his knees in front of me and places his hand on my shoulder. "Don't mess this up for Dad. Go take a shower. The Wellingtons will be here within the hour."

"Only if you get in the shower with me," I say to see how he will respond.

4

His eyes lower for a moment as he breathes harder through his nose. "C'mon, D." He scrubs a hand across his jaw. "We talked about this."

"You want me, too." I slide my hand beneath his chin, forcing him to look at me. "Stop denying it, Bash."

"What we do in the dark can never see the light." He pushes himself up from the ground and extends his hand to me. "Let's go. You need to change."

I take his hand and rise to my full height, our foreheads so close they almost touch. He doesn't step back like usual when we get too close. So I slip my fingers between his and pull him toward me.

"Damian," he mutters.

"Bash." I stare into his eyes, my heart pounding so hard it's about to punch a hole through my chest. "Come upstairs with me. We can turn out the lights."

What we do in the dark can never see the light, Bastian tells me all the time. At least once a week. But it doesn't stop me from wanting him.

He's still holding my hand, thinking about my request. We stand at the cliff's edge for the longest minute before he speaks.

"Okay," he agrees. "But we're going to The Mansion this weekend."

Our father owns a sex club an hour from our house. Since we turned sixteen, he's let us go there whenever we want. And anytime Bash touches me, or me him, he has to purge his dirty deeds at The Mansion. He thinks a woman's pussy will somehow cleanse him of our sins.

"What the fuck are you doing?" Luca shouts from the veranda, dressed in a black suit, looking older than his age. "Are you holding hands? Jesus, fuck. You two are weird."

Our adoptive brother walks toward us, and Bastian releases his grip on my hand. He stands a few feet away like he's sickened by what almost happened.

Again.

I rarely touch anyone but Bash. When I'm with women, I fuck them from behind and use restraints so our skin never touches. The feel of another person's skin on mine usually makes me sick. It's a side effect of dealing with so many dead bodies. After a while, skin is repulsive, especially when you know how it feels cold and lifeless.

But with Bash, the world is brighter. My usual shades of black and gray transform into technicolor when we're together.

"I was just helping Damian get cleaned up," Bastian says, unable to hold Luca's gaze.

"Uh-huh." Luca rolls his eyes. "Sure you were."

He never believes anything we tell him. Luca knows what we do when alone and pretends it's not happening. I don't think he cares one way or the other as long as we keep fucking girls and doing whatever he wants.

Marcello joins us, wearing a suit, with his usually messy black hair slicked off his forehead. He's younger than Luca by eighteen months and yet could be his twin. They have the same jaw, Roman nose, and dark blue eyes they got from their mother, except Marcello is more muscular.

"Wellington and his stupid fucking heirs will be here soon," Luca hisses, his tone laced with venom. "I hate her already, and I've only seen pictures of her."

Alexandrea Wellington might be the prettiest girl I have ever seen. None of us have met in her person. But if she looks anything like her surveillance photos, she's a fucking knockout. The kind of girl so beautiful and pure, I want to taint her.

Ruin her.

"You have to marry her," Bastian says with a light shrug. "At least Wellington's granddaughter is hot. You don't have to like her to fuck her." He grabs his dick over the front of his pants and groans. "And she's a virgin. So if you don't want that tight pussy, I'm taking her cherry."

Luca is the oldest and will probably marry Alex. But her grandfather is giving her a choice between us. If she chooses Bastian or me, it will fuck over our adoptive family and ruin everything. So it's our job to make sure Alex hates us the most.

"I have a better idea," Luca says with a mischievous grin. "I want the three of you to do everything I would have done to her." His eyes flick between us. "Torture her. Make her scream. While I watch."

I kill people.

Luca hurts people.

Bastian saves them.

Marcello protects them.

Luca and I are the most fucked up, beyond deranged, and not quite human anymore. Our souls are black and tainted. But at least I feel something for Bash.

I can't say the same for Luca. He feels nothing for no one, not even his father. But I understand it's because of all the abuse he endured after his mother died.

He hates Marcello, despite saving him from their father as kids. If they didn't look like twins, you would never know they're brothers, not when they act like enemies.

"Leave Alex alone," Marcello says. "She's had a shitty life. This isn't her fault."

"She's had a shitty life?" Luca laughs, but it's sinister and laced with anger. "We've lost everything that fucking matters because of her family."

"It's not her fault," Marcello insists. "She may look like Savannah. But she's not her mother, Luca."

Alex is the granddaughter of one of the Elders of The Founders Society and the third wealthiest man in the world. But until a few days ago, she was Alexandrea Fox and lived a life of poverty. Her mother was disowned and cast out of Devil's Creek.

Now, she's the heir to billions and a pawn in our twisted game. The poor girl thinks she's been saved from her former life. Quite the opposite. Because once we get our hands on her, she'll be just as fucked up as the four of us.

Luca snarls at Marcello. "Her bitch mother killed ours. And she's going to pay for it."

Chapter Two

BASTIAN PUSHES ME INTO THE TILED WALL, WATER SPLASHING our faces. "You're so dirty," he mutters, his hand sliding up my throat. "Why'd you have to go and make a mess before the Wellingtons arrive?" His lips trail down my jaw. "Luca is going to be pissed if we're late."

I tilt my head to the side as he kisses my neck. "You like me dirty."

"Yeah." He smiles against my skin and tugs on my flesh, knowing how much I like the pain. "I wouldn't want you any other way."

This is the closest we ever come to kissing. And if I turn my head and make the first move, I already know what he'll do. The entire moment will be ruined, and he'll pull away from me.

So I don't move.

I let Bastian kiss everywhere but my lips while he fists my cock, which thickens with each stroke. He's not always this affectionate with me. Sometimes, he gets in his head and won't let me touch him. It seems like he only wants me when I'm doing bad shit and wants to fix me.

Today is different.

I can feel it.

I wonder if it has anything to do with us meeting Alexandrea Wellington. Bash called dibs since Luca doesn't want her. For some reason, she gives Bash hope. I'm not sure why, but she does. And if Bash wants her, then so do I. I want anything he wants because I can't lose him.

"Choke me," I bite out since his grasp on my throat is loosening the closer he gets to coming. "Harder," I say when it's still not enough.

His fingers curl around my throat, making it much harder to breathe. And with the loss of oxygen comes the intense orgasm building inside me, my balls aching and begging for a release.

"Is this hard enough, you sick fuck?" Bastian looks into my eyes right before he licks the water from my cheek. "Huh? Tell me how much you hate it when I do this."

I can't.

Because I don't.

I love it.

But he hates himself for getting turned on by me. Maybe we'll find the right girl who can fix us someday. All we need is someone who will accept us exactly how we are. And then, Bash will stop judging himself.

Bastian grunts in my ear as he comes in my hand, his entire body trembling. His grip on my throat loosens, but it's okay because I'm coming too, splashing my cum all over his stomach.

He steps back, and I watch my cum drip down his ripped stomach and onto his cock. His body is absolute perfection—like someone sculpted him by hand.

I lick my lips, staring at his dick before returning my gaze to his face. My cock is already getting hard again, thinking about how badly I want to fuck him.

To *feel* him.

I've had sex with many beautiful women, but I want him more than anyone. Maybe it's because he won't let me fuck him. The hunter in me loves the chase—the thrill of the hunt. And with Bash, I'm always begging him for more.

I never get enough.

As we get rewashed, I move behind him and rub the soap up and down his dick. I nibble on his neck. "I'm so fucking obsessed with you."

He pushes my hand away and spins around to face me. "We're going to be late." I scowl in response, and he adds, "Don't give me that look. Dad will be pissed if we're not downstairs in the next fifteen minutes."

I rest my forehead against his, the water drizzling down our skin and into our eyes. "I need you, Bash. I need *this*. Just give me a few more minutes in our little bubble before we have to pretend that we're different people."

"C'mon, D," he groans, stepping back. "I already got you off. What more do you want from me?"

He acts this way almost every time we fuck around. In the heat of the moment, he goes with the flow. But once we both come, he lets the other head do the thinking for him.

"Everything." I instantly feel the loss of his body heat and hate that he's keeping his distance from me. "I want all of you."

"We don't need a marriage to get into The Founders Society," Bastian says with sadness in his gray eyes that soften them around the edges. "But this is important to our family."

I consider his words for a moment. Without Arlo Salvatore adopting us, we would have had miserable lives. We probably would have been forced to live with Bastian's grandfather. And after only three weeks with him after our parents' death, I thought I was going to lose my mind.

The old bastard is the meanest piece of shit I have ever met. And that's saying a lot coming from me. For fucks sake, I kill people and feel no remorse. And Fitzy is even more sadistic than me.

"We'll go to The Mansion on Saturday." He clutches my face and smiles. "Just you and me. We'll fuck all the women we can get our hands on."

Bash is an entirely different person at the sex club. He

lowers his inhibitions and doesn't think about what we're doing. If only I could get him to stop fearing what sex would mean between us.

"Sure," I bite out. "Whatever makes you feel less disgusted by what we're doing."

He shuts off the water, turning his back to me with a sigh. I stare at his muscular ass for a moment, wondering how my cock will look shoved between his cheeks. All I can do is dream. Because until Bash stops hating himself, I'll never get to fuck him.

He'll never fuck me.

It doesn't matter that I'd sell my soul to the fucking Devil to have his cock inside me. There is no amount of begging that will get me what I want.

I can't even pay for it.

Bastian owns half of Atlantic Airlines, the same as me. Once we're old enough to collect our trust funds, we'll run the company our parents started together.

We're not just adoptive brothers and best friends. This is a marriage between us. Our lives are so intertwined I can't untangle myself from him. So if Carl Wellington's granddaughter gives Bash hope for a different life, then I want that for us.

I want him.

I want her.

I want an *us*.

I follow Bastian out of the shower and towel dry my hair, my eyes on his body that's sculpted to perfection. "Do you think Alex can fix us?"

Bastian dabs at his wet skin and wraps the towel around his waist. "I think she'll be more accepting of us. She's had a rough life and won't judge us. I have a feeling about her. A good one."

I haven't given much thought to her. Not when she's

supposed to marry Luca or Marcello. Alex can't choose Bastian or me. It would fuck up everything for our family.

"Is that why you're so excited about meeting her?"

He rolls his broad shoulders and smiles. "I can't explain it, D. Call it intuition. Alex is the one for us. She's from the right bloodline. One my grandfather approves of."

It's always about his grandfather's approval. Fitzgerald Archibald Adams IV is the reason Bash hates himself so much. He's the one person standing in my way.

"We both need more," Bash adds. "I think you know that."

"I'd miss fucking women if it were only the two of us," I admit as we leave the bathroom and enter my room. "But I would be okay with only fucking you for the rest of my life."

He slips into a pair of boxers and yanks them up his thighs. "I love pussy more than almost anything," he shoots back with a wicked grin. "I need to fuck women. I'm not giving that up. There's nothing better than being balls deep in a wet, tight cunt."

"Yeah," I agree because it's all I have ever known. "But I think I like killing people one-tenth more than sex. If I can have sex after a kill, that's the sweet spot. Nothing gets my dick harder."

"Oh, I know how hard your dick gets over blood," he says with a wink. "Now think about how hard you'd get licking Alex's bloody pussy after I take her virginity."

"Mmmm…" I lick my lips, staring at his mouth as excitement flares inside me. The monster hums to life, begging to come out and play. "Now, we're talking. Even better if you let me suck her blood off your dick. I want it all."

Bash enters the walk-in closet, grabs one of my Brioni suits from the hanger, and sets it on the bed. "Get dressed. We don't have much time before Dad comes looking for us."

"If you want Alex," I say as I strip the jacket off the hanger. "Then why are you going along with Luca's plan to ice her out and make her feel unwanted? It will be easier to get into her pants if you turn on the charm."

When he wants to, Bastian can be very fucking charming. Almost too perfect, if you ask me. He's so good at bullshitting people it sometimes makes me jealous that he has such a natural ease.

Words are easy for him.

On the other hand, I have no social skills whatsoever. I don't understand societal norms or give a fuck either. I look to Bastian and my brothers to help me understand the world.

They help me survive.

After I get dressed in the suit, I accompany Bash to his bedroom on the other side of the wall from mine. He quickly tugs on the fabric, looking fucking amazing in a black Tom Ford suit that clings to his muscles.

Fuck, I want him.

My cock hardens at the sight of him looking so damn good, and I lick my lips, reaching down to fix the bulge in my pants.

Bastian's eyes lower. "Get rid of that now," he scolds like I'm a child. "Fuck, Damian. Do you ever think about anything else?"

"Not when you're in the room."

"I'll tell you what." He inches toward me and fists my tie in his hand, pulling me so close our lips almost touch. If only he would press his lips to mine and stop overthinking. "If you do as I say and don't mess up this meeting with the Wellingtons for us, I'll reward you later for being a good boy."

I like the sound of this.

A sly grin pulls at the corners of my mouth. "Tell me what you want me to do."

Chapter Three

THE WELLINGTONS ARRIVE AT SEVEN O'CLOCK ON THE DOT. Carl Wellington III strolls into the sitting room, dressed in a black tailored suit, his white hair styled with gel. He smells of a musky cologne that reminds me of a Jean Patou fragrance Bash sometimes wears. It has a hint of sandalwood and jasmine.

Alexandrea, who goes by Alex, is attached to her grandfather's right side, her twin brother on his left. They're identical in every way, with the same blonde, curly hair and big, blue eyes that practically jump off their faces. Their skin has a sun-kissed glow that looks natural. And while Alex is about seven or eight inches shorter than me, her brother is well over six feet.

Alex's curls hang over her shoulders and brush the tops of her breasts. She's petite and looks like she hasn't eaten a proper meal in years. But even with her lithe frame, she has decent size tits. Definitely more than a handful.

She's wearing a red strapless dress that stops below her knees, paired with black Louboutin pumps accentuating her thin legs. I hadn't paid much attention to the pictures of her, but Alex is a fucking knockout. Like a younger version of Kate Hudson.

Bash was drooling over the surveillance photos Luca showed him. So was Marcello. I didn't think I could ever factor into this equation and dismissed her as an option.

Luca or Marcello has to marry her. It's the only way to make the Salvatores more legitimate in the eyes of The Founders Society.

However, now that I know she could get me closer to Bash, I want her too. Maybe even more than he does. And why wouldn't I? I would have to be blind not to see her beauty.

"Arlo," Carl says to our father, who steps forward to greet his old friend with a firm handshake. "I'd like you to meet my grandchildren. Aiden and Alexandrea."

"Welcome to Devil's Creek," Dad says with a forced smile.

Aiden tips his head at us, stuffing his hands into his pockets like he doesn't know what to do with them. "Hey!"

He seems uncomfortable in a suit and tie. Carl dressed him up to look like he belongs in this world, born into wealth and privilege. But it's so obvious he wasn't.

"Hi," Alex beams as she shakes our father's hand, not knowing her mom killed his wife in a jealous rage. "I'm so excited to meet you. Your wife inspired so much of my work. I took up painting after my therapist introduced me to her art."

Dad shakes her hand. "That's so lovely to hear, Alexandrea. My Eva would have been thrilled to meet you... if she had lived," he says with his dark eyes aimed at Carl.

Our dad will never forgive Carl for letting his daughter overstep her boundaries. He will never let him forget that his daughter killed his wife. Arlo Salvatore loves few things more than money, and Eva was one of them.

After she died, our home became a nightmare. The abuse started shortly after Eva's funeral, and Luca took the brunt. He has the most scars but hasn't bothered to hide them with tattoos as I did. Even Bash and Marcello covered some of theirs.

Most of my body is inked, leaving only the places you can see when I'm wearing a suit untouched. Our father didn't care if we got ink as long as no one could see it. And over time, it became more about expressing my feelings than hiding the scars.

Aiden stands beside his grandfather, but Alex is braver and approaches us. "Hi." She gives us an adorable smile that touches her pretty blue eyes. "I'm Alexandrea. But you guys can call me Alex. My grandfather says we're in the same grade at school."

"Not the same as me," Marcello responds. "I'm two grades below my brothers."

She nibbles on her lip, shifting her weight to the other foot. "Well, okay. Cool. I guess I'll see you at school then."

He nods, then extends his hand. "I'm Marcello."

A smile tips up the corners of her lips, painted with red lipstick to match her dress. She's so fucking pretty that it makes my chest hurt staring at her. And so innocent. I will enjoy breaking her in, showing her everything I like while Luca watches us.

"Nice to meet you, Marcello." She shakes his hand and then glances at Luca, waiting for him to introduce himself. "And you must be Luca." Her gaze shifts between them. "Has anyone ever told you that the two of you could be twins? You look so much alike."

"No," Luca snaps. "Can't say they have."

It's obvious when you meet Luca and Marcello that they're brothers. Their hatred for one another will make this an interesting competition. Luca is the oldest and should be entitled to marry Alex after college. But, Alex is getting a choice between us, the only kindness her grandfather is giving her.

She gives up trying to be nice to Luca and moves on to Bash. But, unlike Marcello, Bash won't defy Luca's orders and speak to her. Before we got into the shower, Luca said, *If any of you dare talk to her, I'll break your fingers and shove them down your throat so you can't speak again.*

I'm not afraid of Luca.

Neither is Bash or Marcello.

But Bash and I have learned it's best to go with the flow in this house. Luca always gets his way, so there's no point in rocking the boat unless necessary.

"Hi." Alex smiles at Bash and gives him a tiny wave, the blush spreading across her cheeks. She steps closer, staring into his eyes. "You have really pretty eyes. They remind me of slate."

Toying with the cuff bracelet on her wrist, she waits for a response. I can already tell she likes Bash. Or maybe she's one of those people who become overly friendly when they're nervous.

Bastian knows better than to respond. So he nods and turns his head away, looking bored by this meet and greet. But I know Bash well enough to see that it's killing him not to talk to her.

"Okay," Alex whispers, shaking her head. "What's with all the mood swings?"

Alex stops before me, taking in my face as if trying to imprint the image into my mind. "Have you ever let anyone paint you?"

I'm so startled by her question that I stare.

Blink.

"Well?" Alex prompts. "Have you?"

I shake my head.

I can't talk to her because I'm afraid of fucking this up for my brothers… and because Bastian will reward me later for following Luca's orders. This meeting has to go exactly as planned for me to get what I want.

"Your face is perfectly symmetrical," she says with a sweet smile. "I would love to paint you."

Most people take one look at my eyes and run away. Even Bash says there's something about my stare that's terrifying. A dead look that screams, *No one is home.* The smart ones know when they're staring at a predator.

But she's…

Different.

Alex storms off and joins her family. She flicks her blonde curls over her shoulder and sighs. "They're so mean," she says in a hushed tone to her grandfather, but her voice carries in the quiet room. "I tried to be nice, Pops. What did I do wrong?"

Nothing.

She's perfect.

Flawless.

But she'll never understand our motives until she discovers why her grandfather even agreed to this arranged marriage. Our anger and hatred won't make sense until then.

All in due time.

"Fuck them," Aiden says with disdain in his tone, his eyes aimed at us. "They need you more than you need them, Lexie."

He calls his twin Lexie, but the name doesn't match. You know when you meet someone and think, *She doesn't look like a Mary?* Well, that's how I feel about Aiden calling her Lexie.

"You will marry one of the Salvatore boys," Carl Wellington snaps, his tone stern and cold, devoid of emotion, "and it's not up for debate. I saved you from a life of poverty and abuse. Just remember, you owe me, Alexandrea."

"Of course." She lowers her head like a servant instead of the heir to billions. "I'm grateful for everything you have done for us. I won't let you down."

Chapter Four

I LIKE WATCHING HER SQUIRM. EVEN WHEN SHE DOESN'T KNOW I'm looking, I watch *her*. Alex has become my new obsession, and since Luca wants her to feel every ounce of his pain, it's my job to inflict it.

To make her bleed.

When I'm done with her, she'll wish her grandfather never brought her to Devil's Creek. It only took one night to drain the life from her beautiful face. She had so much hope in her eyes when she introduced herself to us. Poor girl thought she would find friends here.

Not a fucking chance.

As she walks the hallways at school, alone and scared, she has no idea I'm following her.

Watching her.

Waiting.

A few days ago, her grandfather adopted Alex and her twin brother, taking them away from their abusive parents. I bet they expected a new life. A better life. But Carl Wellington only saved them from one version of Hell and threw them headfirst into another.

She doesn't belong here.

She knows it.

Feels it.

Luca told everyone in town she was coming and to steer clear of her at Astor Prep. Students pass her with curious looks like she's a circus freak. No one with any common sense speaks to her.

They know better.

Luca is the king of this school. Anyone stupid enough to defy him will pay the price for their insubordination.

Alex is scared.

Fragile.

I study her as she stops in front of her locker and bites her nails. It's a gross habit I will need to break. She doesn't know what I have planned for her. All the ways I will ruin her. And I will enjoy teaching her.

Training her.

Like a good Pet.

Throughout the morning, no one acknowledges her. Not even the teachers. They let her blend into every class as if she were the furniture.

The student body fears the wrath of the Salvatore brothers. So do the staff. They know better than to get in our way. Not unless they want to become a casualty of war.

Alex tried to make friends with a few girls. But they looked the other way when she introduced herself. Only the football team captain dared to defy Luca's order. But Luca shut that shit down real quick.

When the bell rings, Bastian joins me, leaning against the wall across from the bank of lockers. "She's fucking hot." He scrubs a hand across his jaw and sighs. "And she's ours."

"Luca will change his mind."

He shakes his head. "Not a chance. Her mom killed his. There's too much bad blood between them. His dick would probably fall off if he tried to fuck her."

I snort at Bastian's stupid comment. "He hates her now... but I doubt it will last long. Look at her."

My gaze falls on her tight ass that looks perfect in a mid-length skirt. She's skinny and could use more meat on her bones, but that's only because her parents never fed her.

That's okay.

We'll fatten her up.

Luca likes his girls thicker and won't touch her while she's sickly thin. So he'll make sure she is properly nourished.

Blonde curls trail down her back, and when she swings her head to the side, shoving the hair over her shoulder, I nearly lose my mind. She has the face of a fucking angel. And pretty soon, she'll be corrupted by the devil.

She's mine.

Alexandrea Wellington is the best gift Luca has ever given me.

He treats me like I'm a child because of what he calls my affliction. But he has his issues and doesn't have room to judge me. Sometimes, I hate him for being a dick. And for always bossing me around.

But he gave *her* to me.

So we're even.

"I'm trying hard not to go over there and fuck her on the floor like an animal." I lick my lips and glance at Bastian to see he's doing the same thing. "We should tag team her. Break in both of her tight holes at the same time."

We love fucking women together. It's the only time I feel connected to Bash in *that* way. He won't let me fuck him. I can touch his dick and put it in my mouth, but he never crosses the line. He's so afraid that it will make him gay.

And no kissing on the lips.

He has so many fucking rules about us it makes my head spin. But fuck if I care. I want him and will take him any way I can.

"I'm taking her cherry." A creepy smile stretches across his lips. "And if you're a good boy, I'll let you lick the blood from her pussy. But you have to behave yourself, Damian. You can't lose your shit in front of her."

I can't be myself.

The predator.

The hunter.

My eyes flicker with excitement, and my skin tingles, set on fire by the thought of tasting her blood. Adrenaline floods my veins, making my heart race.

I like blood.

The taste.

The smell.

The texture.

"Don't talk to me like I'm a dog," I snap at him. "You and Luca need to cut that shit out."

"I know how you get with blood, D." He gives me one of his shit-eating grins. "Not every girl bleeds a lot when they lose their virginity. But if she does, you better behave." Bash tosses a wink at me. "You know what I mean."

Yeah, I do.

The more blood I see, the worse I get. He's been there for some of the kills. Bastian has even sat beside me while I chopped a body into pieces. Our adoptive father uses my sick need to kill to dispose of his enemies.

Our enemies.

He calls them justified kills. Arlo Salvatore is a sick and twisted man who uses his sons to do his bidding. When he adopted us, it was with a purpose. To use us for our last names in case his plans to leverage a marriage to get into The Founders Society didn't work.

The final bell sounds, and Alex shuts her locker.

"Let's go." Bastian tugs on my jacket. "We'll show our girl to her table. I'm starving."

He grabs Alex's wrist and drags her down the hallway toward the cafeteria. Alex swats at his muscular arm, doing her best to peel his hand from her body, but it's useless.

Why does she even fight back?

Bastian releases a dark chuckle. "Stop fighting me, Cherry."

Her eyes narrow at him, lip quivering. "My name isn't Cherry, asshole."

He stares at her for a moment and then winks. "It is now."

Bastian forces her to sit at our table.

Luca gives Alex a menacing look as Bash shoves her into the chair. Students keep their distance from us, leaving the tables on each side open. We have ruled for the past four years, instilling fear into everyone.

Alex is the only person without the last name Salvatore allowed to sit at our table. She has no idea this is a privilege— an honor to eat with us.

This is our last year at Astor Prep. And after we graduate, we'll leave for The Devil's Knights initiation. Our father is the leader of the secret society. So it's our birthright to become Knights. We're like Masons, but we kill people and do illegal shit for profit.

Luca slides a tray across the table at Alex, his blue eyes colder than ice. "Eat. I'm not fucking a skinny twig."

She glances down at the sandwich on the plate and scowls like the food is poisoned. And to my surprise, she pushes the tray at him.

"I wouldn't fuck you if you paid me."

Maybe she's not so weak after all.

All conversation in the room comes to a screeching halt. Everyone stares at her, shocked by her outburst.

Stupid girl.

Luca's jaw ticks and he glares at her as if he might reach across the table and snap her neck. I hope he doesn't because I like staring at her. She's beautiful. And I want to feel her body tremble each time I touch her.

I want to mark her.

Own her body.

"I don't care if you're a Wellington." Luca is out of his chair in seconds. "That name means absolutely nothing to me. In this town, *Salvatore* is the only name that matters." He points at the space in front of him on the floor. "Get over here."

She shakes her blonde head, curls framing her heart-shaped face. "Dream on."

Luca rounds the table, nostrils flared. Alex tries to escape, but Luca is quicker and fists her hair in his palm.

He yanks her up from the chair. "Wanna try that again, Wellington whore?"

She elbows him in the stomach, and I love that she's a fighter. My dick is already hard and tenting my slacks. I reach under the table and stroke myself, not giving a single fuck we're being watched.

Alex stomps on Luca's foot. "I'm not a whore."

His eyes widen with rage. I can't tell if he's as turned on as me or if he might kill her in front of everyone.

She has no idea why he hates her so much. I wonder how she'll react when she discovers the truth about her fucked up family. Knowing her mother murdered Luca and Marcello's mother will crush her spirit.

The great Evangeline Franco was a world-renowned painter and celebrity in the art world. She is also Alex's favorite artist and idol.

But I hated her.

My adoptive mother never liked me. She treated me like trash before her death. The woman didn't even take the last name Salvatore when she married Arlo.

I don't miss her.

She was a bitch.

Eva would have sent Bash and me to live with someone else if she were still alive. We were parentless and homeless, and Arlo wanted to keep us. They fought over it all the time.

The world believes Evangeline died in a car accident. Which means Alex does, too. But that was all staged by The Founders to cover up the truth.

Alex squirms, but Luca ignores her and palms the back of

her head until her knees hit the floor. "Kiss my boots like a good little slave."

With Alex on her knees, I resist the urge to whip out my cock and shove it past her pretty lips.

She's so fucking sexy.

Luca is controlled on the outside but is close to losing it. He won't touch her, but he wants her. I can see the desire masked as hatred plastered on his face. Wanting her is making him miserable. Since she arrived in Devil's Creek, he's been a horrible asshole to all of us.

Alex shakes her head. "Never. I did nothing wrong."

"You exist," Luca fires back. "That's enough."

"Why do you hate me so much?"

"Ask your grandfather." Luca smirks. "See if he'll tell you the truth about why you're *really* here."

Luca walks away and raises his hand to beckon a blonde girl with huge tits. Stacey Carlton has the same blonde, curly hair and blue eyes as Alex. But where Stacey has more curves, Alex has the face of a model.

She's gorgeous.

My brother is going to use Stacey to get back at Alex. And judging by the look on Alex's face, his plan is working. She almost seems sad, like she would rather have Luca use her instead.

As Luca leaves with Stacey, Alex rises from the floor, fixing her hair and unable to take her eyes off them.

My Pet is jealous.

Luca glances over his shoulder at Alex before he leaves the room and grabs Stacey's ass.

I know he'll think about Alex when he comes in Stacey's mouth. But Alex doesn't know that.

Chapter Five

Luca has been rubbing Stacey in Alex's face all week. If she as much as looks at him during lunch, he yanks Stacey out of her chair and puts on a show.

On Wednesday, Luca made the queen bee of Astor Prep blow him at our table and forced Alex to watch. He's never done that before.

Not until she showed up.

Of course, Alex tried to ignore him. But curiosity must have gotten the best of her because she locked eyes with him until he came into Stacey's mouth.

Alex and Luca have a weird connection that doesn't need words. The rest of the room pretended it wasn't happening. But she looked him dead in the eyes and bit her lip until he finished, hand balled into a fist on the table.

She was mad it wasn't her.

It's all part of our plan to break Alex down. To fuck with her mind and make her question her sanity. Because one day, she's going to be *ours*. Another thing she doesn't know yet.

I meet Bastian at the bank of lockers after fifth period. No one is allowed to have a locker on this wall, a special request our father made to the headmaster. Whatever we want, he finds a way to get it for us.

And we want privacy.

Well, we need it.

Our family makes most of our money legitimately. But the

Salvatores were once in the Italian Mafia. From Sicily to the United States, we have connections. But our father refused to join a crime family. Instead, he founded Salvatore Global. He's the master of secrets and used his power and influence to build a multi-billion dollar private security company.

"What took you so long?" Bastian turns his head to look at me while he digs for something in his locker. "You were supposed to get out of class five minutes early."

I shrug. "Fell asleep in the middle of the lecture. Didn't even know the class was over until Mrs. Finkle tapped me on the shoulder and scared the shit out of me." I shake my head, laughing at the memory. "I almost knocked that old bitch on her ass."

Bash laughs. "She should know better than to sneak up on a sleeping tiger."

I enter the combination into the lock and open the door. There's not much inside, only the essentials. A set of hunting knives. Ropes and zip ties. A shovel and drop cloths. You never know when you need to kill someone. And it's best to have the right tools if the need arises.

Astor Prep doesn't use textbooks, so we have little inside our lockers. Everything is digital, and all of the homework is submitted online. Even our tests are taken on computers.

I grab a stick of gum from the pack and fold it onto my tongue. The mint soothes me. My therapist says certain sounds, smells, and tastes can elicit different responses in the brain.

But he doesn't know the true depths of my darkness. He has no idea my urges are not just sexual. That my soul is blacker than coal, and I have no feelings for anyone or anything other than Bash.

He thinks he's treating me for a raging sex addiction. But, little does the old man know, I'm a serial killer. I have killed over thirty people in the past two years and feel zero remorse. They were pieces of shit who deserved to die.

I would kill them again.

Something warm splashes the back of my pants and dress shoes. It hits Bash, too. A coffee cup drops to the floor at our feet.

"Oops," a girl says with laughter in her voice. "My bad. I'm so clumsy."

Alex.

Furious, I threw out my arm to block her path. She's going to fucking pay for this. Our little pawn thinks she's so clever. From day one at this school, she's acted like she can do whatever she wants. But we owned her the second she moved to Devil's Creek.

Bastian grits his teeth and tugs on the gold tie hanging loosely around his neck. "Clean it up. Now."

Alex gets in his face. "Make me."

I push down on her head to force her to kneel. "Lick the coffee off our shoes."

She smacks my hand away, surprisingly strong for a girl who needs to gain another twenty pounds not to look emaciated. "Fuck you!"

"Stick out your tongue, Pet," I growl, hoping she keeps talking back. "Or you'll be sucking my dick instead."

She slides backward across the tile so she's out of my grasp. It's funny how she assumes we're going to let her go.

Alex rises to her full height, pushing out her chest. "If you put your dick near my mouth, I'm biting it off."

If only she knew what the future holds for her. She's going to be sucking all of our dicks in no time. We have plans for our Wellington prize, including breaking her in every way possible.

But what's even more exciting about Alex is that she's already broken. Her bitch mom did that for us. She locked her in closets and made her fear the dark. But she'll soon find out we not only live in the dark, we thrive in it.

31

"You're ours to command." An evil smirk tugs at Bastian's mouth. "Ours to break."

She tips her head back and laughs. But we're not laughing. And we don't find what she did the least bit funny.

Alex scoffs at the idea. "Not a chance."

"Fight us," Bastian challenges with fire behind his words. "We like playing with our food."

She attempts to walk away, and Bastian latches onto her arm, yanking her backward and into his chest. "Where do you think you're going, Cherry? We're not done with you."

Bastian decided he'd never call her by name.

"I'm not touching either of you," she says like she has a choice. "So you might as well quit while you're ahead." Her pretty blue eyes flick back to Bastian. "And stop calling me Cherry."

He slams his locker.

In one swift motion, Bastian pins Alex's arms above her head, holding her against the locker. He makes room for me, knowing I want in on the action.

I step forward and run my hand up her inner thigh, shoving up her skirt for anyone in the hallway to see. I'm blocking most of the view with my body, but still, someone could catch a glimpse.

My heart pounds with each inch I take closer to her pussy. Her chest rises and falls as our eyes meet, her breathing labored. I enjoy making people uncomfortable.

It's my specialty.

Most people say I freak them out. I make them feel weird because I rarely speak and mostly stare. Bastian says my death glare could scare the Devil back to Hell. He worries I'll snap, and he'll lose me. His biggest fear is abandonment after losing everyone he loves.

Everyone but me.

As my hand inches higher, a whimper escapes Alex's plump lips. She likes how this feels. I can tell by the desire lighting up her eyes, the hardening of her nipples through the white dress shirt.

But she also hates herself for liking how I make her feel. This is something she shares with Bash. They both want me and deny themselves.

I bunch the soft fabric around Alex's hips while Bash holds her tighter. Her black pump falls onto the floor. And I take a second to savor the feel of her soft skin as I wrap her leg around me. Bastian lets go of her hands, and my eyes drop to his cock.

He wants her, too.

Fuck, I want them both.

Bastian moves behind Alex and presses his big cock into her ass while I mold my chest to hers. Sandwiched between us, she has nowhere to run. And we like her at our mercy.

She better remember later when she's complaining to her twin brother that she started it. We would have left her alone if she hadn't dumped coffee on us.

This is on her.

I bet she's wet and ready for us, so I push her panties to the side.

"Damian," she whimpers.

People whisper on the other side of the hallway, our names floating from their mouths. Everyone talks about us. It doesn't matter if we're at school or shopping in town. The Salvatores and the other founders of Devil's Creek are always the topics of conversation among these nosy assholes.

Keeping my focus on Alex, I lick my lips and use my finger to test her wetness, dragging it down her slit.

Fuck, she's so wet.

Soaked.

I repeat the same motion several times until she moans for me.

That's it, Pet.

Sing for me.

She closes her eyes, and I smirk when she opens them again.

I pry her lips open and stuff my finger into her mouth. "Suck it."

She follows my order and takes my finger into her mouth. Goddamn, I can't wait to fuck all of her holes.

"Are you sorry, Cherry?" Bash buries his face in her neck, his teeth grazing her skin. "Answer me."

"No," she mutters. "This changes nothing. I still hate both of you."

Bastian flashes a set of pearly white teeth and chuckles. "Your pussy says otherwise."

I stare at her beautiful face, considering my next move. Not like I care about getting to class, but the bell is about to ring. She needs to maintain her grades, or she won't have the GPA she needs to get into the fancy art school Luca is pulling strings for her to attend in the fall.

Despite being a bunch of mean assholes, we don't hate her. Luca says he does, but his actions prove otherwise. He wouldn't have used his dead mother's name to help Alex get accepted into the Rhode Island School of Design if he hated her.

Evangeline Franco graduated from RISD and became one of the world's most successful painters. And Alex aspires to be just like Evangeline.

"You don't own me," Alex says to me with fire behind her words.

I clutch her chin, smearing her juices on her pretty, pale skin. "Yes, I do."

She's beautiful but not very smart. I'm the last person she wants to fuck with. I'm the least reserved of all my brothers when pushed outside my comfort zone. I could accidentally hurt her in a moment of blind rage or bloodlust.

I think of her body smeared in blood, and a sick feeling

rushes over me. A calming wave that glides over my skin like water spilling onto the beach.

My hunting knives are right there. In my locker. I could easily reach in and grab my leather kit and show her what I *really* like.

Bastian senses my mood and moves out from behind her. He wraps his hand around her throat, pressing his nose to her cheek. "No one is coming to save you." With his free hand, he grabs her pussy. "We own you now, pretty girl."

She rolls her eyes. "No, you don't."

Bastian leans forward and bites her bottom lip, tugging on it with his teeth. "You're here because we willed it. And you will stay in Devil's Creek until we're done playing with you."

"I'm not a toy," she says with conviction. "You can make all the deals you want, but I will never be yours."

I laugh at her feistiness, getting sick of listening to her talk back. So I slide my hand beneath her chin and pull her closer. "If I tell you to suck my cock, you get on your knees like a good little whore."

"I've never done that before," she mutters, not realizing how much this turns me on.

We want to train her.

If she thinks her confession will scare us, she has much to learn about men and their desires. And now that I'm thinking about training my precious Pet, I decide to test her by shoving my fingers into her mouth.

She chokes when I push them back too far.

I laugh.

So does Bash.

"We'll have to work on her gag reflex," I tell Bastian. "This won't do."

"I wouldn't trust your dick anywhere near my mouth," she says, but the words are muffled.

I shake my head. "We're going to teach you, Pet."

"We?"

Bastian laughs. "You think you're getting one of us without the other? Not a chance. All four of us asked for you. Even Marcello wants a piece of Wellington pussy. Our father was happy to oblige."

"Why do you want me?" Alex breathes harder as the panic sets in, looking for an escape route. "You don't even know me."

Because I like touching my Pet, I trace my fingers down the side of her body a few times before my hand settles on her hip. "For the same reason all predators hunt."

"This is a sport to you," she guesses.

The bell rings, and she lets out a breath of air. She's in luck that we don't have any afternoon classes together.

Luca appears from around the bend, reaching down to zip his pants. He's gotten his dick sucked in the middle of the hallway. It doesn't matter to him if anyone sees. I think he secretly likes when people watch him. It only adds to his narcissistic need to be the center of attention.

"Where were you?" Bastian asks him.

He winks. "I put Stacey Carlton's mouth to good use." Luca's eyes land on Alex, a menacing glare in them. "Speaking of mouthy women, how is this one behaving?"

"She's not." Bastian shrugs. "But she'll learn."

"Yes, master," she deadpans.

Good girl.

A satisfied grin tugs at my mouth. "See, she's catching on already."

Chapter Six

SITTING THROUGH MY NEXT CLASS IS UNBEARABLE. EVEN AFTER smoking a blunt with Luca, I still can't get my head on straight. Adrenaline floods my veins like a shot of heroin working through my system.

My hands shake uncontrollably as I reach into my pocket and grab my cell phone. I text Bash with 9-1-1, telling him to meet me in the faculty bathroom, where we will have privacy.

He knows the drill.

Whenever I have urges, he feeds my demons. We can't have people see me lose control, so he does whatever is necessary to help me. This wouldn't have happened if my Pet didn't provoke me. She tossed the coffee at our feet and brought out the monster inside me.

I get an instant response from Bash and slide out of my chair, shoving the phone into my pocket. The teachers know better than to ask where I'm going when I get up and leave in the middle of class. Mr. Houston's eyes lift momentarily and then go back to the whiteboard.

When we first started school at Astor Prep, the teachers tried to control us. But one call from our father to the headmaster squashed that shit real quick. To lose our family's money would be detrimental to this institution.

I power walk down the hallway and rush into the bathroom. My hands tremble so badly I can barely flick open the button of my pants. Leaning against the wall, I wait for

Bastian to enter the room seconds later with the same needy look in his eyes.

I tip my head at the door.

He locks it and approaches me as I unzip my pants and whip out my cock. "I can't stop thinking about her pussy."

He takes in my length and licks his lips. "Same," he agrees, breathing harder. "I'm popping her fucking cherry. I don't care if Luca has a problem with it."

Stroking my shaft, I focus on his mouth and how his lips part for me. I reach out and put his hand around my dick. "This is for you too, Bash. Not just Alex."

He closes his eyes and jerks my dick harder, leaning forward to put his hand on the wall behind my head. "Sometimes, I really hate you, D." His face burrows into the crook of my neck with each stroke, his long fingers sliding up to the tip dripping with precum. "But I can't fucking live without you."

We have a trauma bond, as the therapist calls it. He said our parents' deaths formed an unbreakable bond that's made us codependent on each other. I don't even know how I could be with a woman without him involved.

I need him.

We need each other.

While he rips a grunt from my throat, I unzip his pants and jerk his dick as hard as he's yanking on mine. Like he wants to break it. But fuck, I don't care what he does because it feels good. And I want to cum all over his hand.

My lips press against his earlobe before I suck it into my mouth. His guttural groan pieces my eardrum. I love the sounds Bash makes when he's about to come. They make me feral, and before I know what I'm doing, I'm on my knees in front of him.

He tries to push my head away, but I grab his dick and suck him into my mouth.

"Fuck, D," he moans, his hand falling to the back of my

head. "I hate you so fucking much right now. Why do you do this to me?"

His words don't bother me. I'm used to him denying how he feels. It's the shame talking.

"You're so good at that," he whispers, gripping the ends of my short hair tighter. "Fuck. Why do you have to make me like this?"

I shove down his pants and boxers without losing momentum. They lower to the ground around his ankles, and now I've got a better look at him. His dick is perfect. Thick, long, and big enough to fit him in my mouth.

Squeezing his ass, I deep-throat his dick, taking him all the way down.

"Goddammit," he grunts, tugging so hard on my hair he could pull it from my scalp. "Fuck, Damian. Suck my cock like a good boy."

As I suck his dick, I wipe some of the precum from my tip and use it to lubricate my finger. Bastian falls forward when I plunge my finger into his ass and work the tight channel I've been begging to fuck for the past two years. He likes when I do this, even though he denies me sex.

"Holy shit," he moans. "Fuck, that feels…"

He can't even get out the words, nearly breathless, as I pump my finger into his ass and suck the cum from his dick.

This all started when we were sixteen, and I was out of my mind with bloodlust. I killed someone for my father and lost control. There was so much blood it looked like a massacre. I had blood all over my face, skin, and clothes. Every inch of the floor and walls was painted crimson.

I almost hurt Bastian until he took out my dick and made me come. Because of him, I didn't kill anyone else that night. We went home, got into the shower, and he sucked my dick for the first time.

Then I sucked his.

It was one of the best nights of my life but probably not his. Because that was the night he started hating himself.

And it was all my fault.

Bastian's legs shake, and his grunts quickly turn to sexy moans. His warmth spills into my mouth, and I swallow his cum, licking my lips to get every last drop.

"Jesus," Bastian hisses, his fingers sliding through his dark caramel hair to push it out of his eyes. "No one sucks my dick like you do."

I rise from the ground, still hard and needing a release. So I take his hand and wrap it around my shaft. His hand glides up and down my skin in a rhythmic motion.

"I need to feel your mouth on me, Bash." I stick out my tongue and lick his lips, so he can taste himself. "Make this go away."

Unless I'm lost to the madness, I always take care of him first. It's easier to get Bash out of his head if he comes. He doesn't think as much about our wrongness. How much he hates his feelings for me. But he would have to cut out my black heart to make me stop feeling this way about him.

I've been getting better at knowing my limits over the years. So I can sense when the urges resurface and usually find Bastian in time.

Bash licks the taste of his cum from his bottom lip. For a split second, our eyes meet, and I think he might kiss me. I've tried so many times with him. But he insists on no kissing or fucking.

Apparently, kissing a man would make him gay. But sucking my dick is a gray area for him. Whatever floats his boat. As long as this never ends, I don't fucking care. He can label us with whatever he wants.

Bi.

Gay.

Straight.

Don't care.

I flatten my tongue against his cheek and lick up to the skin beneath his eye. "I *need* you."

The crazier shit I do, the more it lowers his guard. Bastian gives me a hesitant look before getting on his knees and fisting my shaft. I know how to work him over until I get what I want. And he's good at manipulating me, too.

"Suck on your fingers," I tell him.

He does as I request, staring up at me with those big, gray eyes, and then shoves two wet fingers into my ass. "Is this what you want, you crazy fuck?"

His fingers work my tight hole, and even though it burns, I don't care. It feels so fucking good.

I nod and slide the tip of my cock across his lips. "I want to paint your tongue with my cum."

Shaking his head, he sighs. "How did we get here, Damian?"

He wishes he could stop.

But he can't.

"It didn't take much convincing," I point out, my voice muffled as he fucks my ass with his fingers. "You love my dick. So suck it, and stop playing games."

It's the truth.

He's told me plenty of times in the heat of the moment that he loves my dick in his mouth. Loves how I make him feel.

And I know this to be true when he licks playfully up and down my shaft before my cock disappears into his mouth. My fingers slip through his hair. It's a few inches longer than mine, which I like. This way, I can pull harder whenever he tortures me with his mouth.

He looks up at me, holding my gaze, with his cheeks puffed out from fitting all of me. Running my fingers through his hair, I take in the feel of his soft locks and the scent of bergamot in his cologne.

I love everything about him. How he smells, tastes, and

looks. Bastian is perfect in every way. And he's always been there for me.

He protects me. And sometimes, he has to save me from myself.

With two fingers in my ass and the warmth of his mouth driving me fucking crazy, I come so hard and fast that my body jerks like it's been hit by a hurricane.

He pulls back after I fill his mouth with cum and opens up for me. I get off on seeing my cum on his tongue and smile. Bastian knows all the ways to please me.

"You looking fucking hot with my cum in your mouth." I run my thumb across his lip. "I wish you'd fuck me."

He rolls his eyes and swallows, pulling away from me. "Stop with that shit, would ya?" Bastian rises from the floor and wipes his mouth with the back of his hand, turning his head toward the door. "I'm *not* fucking you."

"How is it any different than anal with a woman?" I tuck my dick into my pants and cup his shoulder, forcing him to look at me. "I bet you think of me while you're fucking them in the ass. Don't you? I can see the look in your eyes. Your focus is on me—not them."

"It's not the same." He walks over to the sink and washes his hands, scrubbing so hard his skin could crack open. "And you know it, D."

"Actually, no, I don't." I move to the sink beside him and lather my hands with soap. "Because you won't let me find out."

"Never will." He grabs paper towels and dries his hands. "So get the thought out of your mind."

"You know it will feel good." I turn off the sink and take the extra towel from his hand. "So what's the problem?"

He scoffs. "We're already crossing enough lines. The two of us may not be blood-related, but we are brothers. We are Salvatores. Can you imagine what kind of shame we'd bring to our family if anyone ever found out about us?" Bastian shakes his head, disgusted with himself. "The Founders would never let us into The Society, and Dad would hate us for it."

"Luca and Marcello already know," I say because he seems to need a reminder that our little secret is not so secret anymore. "And if Dad knows, I doubt he cares."

"The answer is no," Bastian snaps, taking one last look in the mirror before unlocking the door and leaving without another word.

Chapter Seven

I NEVER TALKED MUCH AS A CHILD. AND AS AN ADULT, I SPEAK even less. My biological parents couldn't figure out why I rarely communicated using words.

They thought I had a learning disability. Autism. A mental illness. Just about everything the doctors could dig up from their medical journals.

I just didn't like to talk.

Bastian understood me from the start. He's only three months older than me. And since our parents were best friends and founded an airline together, we were inseparable from birth.

We spent almost every day together. Every holiday and birthday. There were very few days we weren't at each other's houses. I even attended all of his concerts.

You wouldn't know it by looking at Bash, but he's a prodigy pianist. He started playing when he was only two years old and still writes music. And some nights, he plays for me when I can't sleep.

I sit on his bed and watch his fingers glide across the keys. He's so graceful when he's playing. Like a dancer getting lost in the beat. An artist allowing the muse to take over.

After he finishes the song, he looks at me and pats the bench. "I wrote something for you."

He hasn't done this in a long time, and excitement rushes through me.

I slide off the bed and sit beside him. "Did you name the song?"

Bash bobs his head. "I'm calling it The Darkest Prince."

People in town call us the princes of Devil's Creek, like we are royalty. And to them, we're the closest you'll get to royalty in America. Our lineage traces back to the Founding Fathers of the United States. That's why Bash and I can join The Founders Society later in life. But our adoptive family needs a marriage to get accepted.

"The Darkest Prince." I smile, a real one that touches my eyes. Smiles are rare for me, but not when I'm with Bash. "It's fitting."

"There's darkness inside you. It was there even before your parents died." His fingers inch closer to mine on the bench. "Luca is the cruelest prince." He laughs. "And Marcello is the protective prince."

I brush the fallen strand of hair off his forehead and look into his eyes. They're gray and remind me of stone. "Which prince are you?"

"The creative prince?" He shrugs. "I don't know. I'm not as mysterious as you. Or as mean as Luca... or as noble as Marcello."

"How about the possessive prince?"

He rolls his broad shoulders again, looking away from me. Our moment of intimacy is too intense. When we're alone, he doesn't usually mind my touch. But I can tell he needs his space. What we did earlier was too much for him. Any more affection tonight will send him into a spiral of self-loathing.

I lower my hand, tapping my fingers nervously on my knee. "Play the song for me."

His fingers sweep across the keys with practiced precision. He's brilliant and brings the haunting sound to life. The tune reminds me of something from The Phantom of the Opera. It's sad and instantly pierces my soul, penetrating my black heart with each keystroke.

When he plays the last note, my heart feels like it's cracking in my chest. I rarely feel anything. With my condition, I don't understand normal human emotions. I have to take most of my social cues from Bash. He helps me understand people and the world since I don't get it.

Bastian angles his body to look at me. "What do you think?"

I'm rendered speechless by his performance. He played as if he were on stage again at one of his concerts. His music is what helped me to open up to him. Music is a form of therapy for both of us.

Bastian learned how to play from his mom. She was supposed to be at his concert the day our parents' plane blew up over the Pacific Ocean. Back then, we thought it was an accident. But we now know terrorists called The Lucaya Group killed them, though their motive remains a mystery.

"Talk to me, D." He waves his hand in front of my face. "You're zoning out on me. Did you hate it?"

I shake my head, finally able to speak. "No, it's perfect." I scoot closer to him on the bench, overcome by a wave of emotions his song produced inside me. "Play it again."

He plays for me until midnight, and then we crawl into his bed. Bastian is the only person who can quiet my night terrors. And after tonight, I'll sleep like the dead.

"Luca said something to me earlier," Bash says once the room is submerged in darkness. "He wants us to share Alex."

"Yeah, I know."

"No, it's not what you think. After college, he'll marry her to satisfy the deal with the Wellingtons and knock her up to get a kid with Founders' blood. But after he gets what he wants, he's done with her."

"What's that have to do with us?"

His fingers find mine on the mattress. "Are you listening to me, D? Luca said we can have *her*. I know that's what you

47

want. I see the way you look at her. You wouldn't have lost control at school if you didn't feel something for her."

There's something about the darkness in Alex that speaks to my soul.

I felt it the night we met.

You can't break someone who's already broken. And I like that about her. She knows what it's like to go through years of trauma only to get fucked over again by life. We have money and power but are still not whole. No amount of money can fix fucked up people.

"I want to keep her," I admit. "But Luca will change his mind. And even if he doesn't, she'll never accept me, not like this. She couldn't handle the dirty parts of my life. A girl like that would run the first chance she got."

"Then we won't let her." His fingers lace between mine. "I have a feeling about her, D. She's right for *us*."

If this girl gives me any chance at having more with Bash, I'm taking it.

No questions asked.

I'm so excited I climb on top of him, pinning his arms to the mattress. My cock is already hard and rubbing against his.

"I want to try something," I say, my lips inches from his.

"If you kiss me," he groans, "I'm going to punch you."

"I'm not going to kiss you," I confirm to alleviate his concern, and his shoulders slump against the bed in relief. "But I want to see how this feels."

His eyes narrow on me. "You're not fucking me either."

"Nope." I shake my head. "Just let me do this. I promise it will feel good."

I slid off him for a second and strip off my boxers, quickly discarding his next. We're both naked, our dicks harder than steel. I lean over the side of the bed and snatch the bottle of lube from his nightstand drawer.

He gives me a weary look as I move between his thighs

and get on top of him, placing my palms on the mattress on each side of his head.

"What are you doing, Damian?"

I grab his hand and reach between us to wrap it around his shaft. Then I repeat the same process with my dick, but I line mine up with his so we're flush against each other.

He's around nine inches, and mine is maybe a half inch bigger, where he's thicker. But together, we fit perfectly.

Bash bites his bottom lip, staring up at me with desire. "I don't get what you're trying to do, D. I'm not a girl."

"For now, this is the closest we'll get to fucking." I take his hand and fold his fingers around the base of both of our dicks. "You stroke us from the bottom," I tell him as I curl my hand around the top of our cocks, gliding over the heads that are wet with precum. "And I'll do the rest."

Balancing myself on my left palm, I open the bottle of lube and drizzle it onto our cocks, getting some of it on our hands. "Get us nice and wet, Bash."

He does as I say and helps me lube our dicks.

"Oh, fuck," Bastian grunts, moving in unison with me, "Jesus, Damian." His eyes slam shut with each thrust. "What the fuck?" He hisses. "I'm not gonna last long."

"Cum all over me, Bash," I bite out as we work each other over in harmony, my skin tingling from head to toe. "Fuck, you feel so good. Make a mess for me."

We're both on the edge, so close to exploding that my balls tighten in response. My entire body tenses up, and a shiver rushes down my spine, slowly spreading down my legs.

"I'm gonna come," Bash chokes out, his gray eyes meeting my green ones. "Fuck."

His chest rises and falls faster than normal the closer we race to the finish line. I can barely catch my breath I'm so fucking turned on, my skin scorching from the inferno blazing inside me.

"Fuck, fuck, fuck," Bash curses as his cum shoots out from

the tip of his cock, some of it hitting my chin. But most of it lands on his stomach.

"Don't stop," I tell him once his grip loosens on me. "I'm right there, Bash. Rub your fat cock against mine until I nut all over you."

His cum drips onto my skin and mixed with the lube, it's even more slippery as we stroke up and down from the base to tip. With us joined like this, we become one. This is the first and only time I have ever felt so close to him.

My cum shoots out of me like hot lava erupting from a volcano. I can hardly control my aim it comes out of me so violently, hitting Bash in the chest. A good amount of it is on the sheets and his bicep.

I collapse on top of him, the two of us covered in our cum and breathing heavily. "Holy shit. I don't think I've ever come that hard before."

"Me neither," he agrees, running his fingers through my short, black hair. "That was... Fuck, D. You never cease to amaze me. I came so fast I felt like I was in middle school all over again."

I laugh. "Felt good, didn't it?"

I need to hear him say it.

"Fuck, yeah." He smiles. "This is the only time I get to see the real you. I like it. That's why I won't stop, even though I can't wrap my head around what we're doing."

"What we do in the dark can never see the light," I say, using his words against him. "But one day, you won't be ashamed of who you are. One day, you'll be mine and won't care what people think."

"One day," he agrees. "Until then, this stays between us."

Chapter Eight

I's been weeks since that day in the hallway with Alex. And since then, she's accepting her place among us like a good little pet. Our girl isn't complacent or compliant, but she doesn't argue. She seems to enjoy being around us.

No more sulking.

No more fights.

Luca has another girl on his lap, throwing her in Alex's face. Stacey is in the chair beside him, planting kisses on his neck while Barbie 2.0 gets on her knees in front of him.

This is the tenth blowjob we have all witnessed during our lunch period since Alex arrived. Luca was never this bad. Sure, he's fucked every cheerleader and most of the girls in the senior class. But what he's doing today isn't about sex.

It's all for show.

Alex's eyes widen when Carrie pulls out Luca's cock. He's a lot bigger than Bash and me and thicker, too. His dick's got to be as long as the girl's forearm.

You can always tell when a girl's a real whore. Carrie eyes up Luca's dick like it's a lollipop and doesn't hesitate to take most of him in her mouth. She gags when he puts his hand on her hand, forcing her to take more of him.

I watch Alex.

So does Bash.

Every time Luca does this, Alex maintains eye contact with him. Her eyes never leave his dark blue ones, so he keeps doing it. This girl's lips are wrapped around his cock. But he's getting off to Alex. I wonder if he can't come anymore unless it's to the thought of her.

Bash and I have been having the same problem. Even the women at The Mansion are not cutting it anymore. So we made a pact not to take Alex's virginity until the right time.

And all of us will honor it.

Alex must be angry at Luca today because she grabs my hand. Then she reaches for Bash's, placing both of our hands on her thighs. She scoots her chair backward, so Luca can get a better look and spreads her legs wider.

"You wanna play, Cherry?" Bastian bends down and flicks his tongue over her earlobe. "We'll help you get even with him."

Her lips part, and without a word, she inches our hands higher up her thighs. She doesn't have to tell me twice. If she wants to get off to Luca getting his dick sucked, we'll help her do it.

We intentionally sit away from the rest of the students. People can see what Luca is doing, but they know better than to look over here. And if anyone tries to film this shit, Luca would snap their neck.

I help Bash hike up Alex's skirt, revealing a pair of pink, lacy panties. They have a little bow that makes her look so damn innocent. She's still a virgin, but this girl was tainted long before she met us.

Alex is bad like us.

I grab the hunting knife from my pocket and tear the panties clean off her sexy body.

Alex yelps. "Hey, what are you doing?"

"You're pretty when you're scared, Pet."

She scoffs. "I'm not afraid of you."

I stuff the fabric in my pocket, and the scent of her pussy is all I can smell in a room full of food aromas. "No, you're intrigued, which is much worse for you. Most people know when monsters are hunting them. But not you, Pet. You want to play with the monsters."

She holds out her hand. "I want my underwear back."

I shake my head. "I'll buy you a closet full of lingerie, so I can keep ripping them off you."

Alex rolls her eyes. "You're sick, Damian."

"Hmmm..." I get close enough to make her squirm. "So I've been told."

"Fuck. Me." Bash grunts, his eyes on her pretty pussy. "You're already wet for us." He nuzzles her neck with his nose and runs his finger down her slit. "Watching Luca get his dick sucked turns you on, doesn't it?"

"Shut up, Bash." She guides my hand between her thighs. "Both of you shut up and touch me before I come to my senses."

I look at Bash, and we can communicate without words with a simple head gesture. Our fingers move inside her, spreading her tight pussy open. I love the feel of his skin rubbing against mine inside her. They feel so fucking good.

"Oh, God," she whimpers.

"Feels good, doesn't it, Cherry?"

She bites her lip and nods.

We pull back our fingers and slam into her again. Cum drips out of her and onto the chair.

"Look at you, Pet." I press my lips to her ear. "Making a mess we'll have to clean up. What do you think we should do about that?"

"I don't care." She grips our arms and glares at Luca with unbridled hatred. "Just don't stop."

A soft moan escapes her throat as we fuck her with our fingers. Her eyes say, *Fuck you. I'm going to use your brothers to make you jealous.*

And it works.

Luca yanks on Carrie's head until his dick pops out of her mouth. He tucks himself back into his boxers and zips his pants, rising to his full height. "Let's go." He snaps his fingers at us. "And bring her with you."

He yanks Carrie up from the floor and shoves Stacey away from our table by smacking her ass. "You bitches better get moving." Then his gaze is on us again. "We'll be waiting for you."

We know what that means, but Alex is clueless. She looks to us for an explanation, which we don't offer. Better to let her find out on her own. This would not be happening if she didn't challenge Luca.

After Luca walks away with the girls, Bastian says, "Bad, Cherry. You poked the dragon. And now he's going to burn down the fucking village."

She moves the skirt down her thighs to cover her pussy. "What he's going to do?"

Bastian gets up from the chair and offers his hand to her, grinning. "You'll see."

Surprisingly, Alex doesn't ask questions and follows us out of the cafeteria. She keeps tugging at the back of her skirt now that she's not wearing panties. So once we're in the empty hallway, I reach under the skirt and grab a handful of her ass.

"No one at this school will ever think about looking at what's ours," I tell her, keeping my hand on her ass cheek as we walk. "This belongs to us."

She doesn't disagree.

Alex wants to be ours.

Even though I can feel the fear shake through her body, she's curious about what will happen. Luca has never been nice to her. The only kindness he offers is food and protection.

No one fucks with her.

No one talks to her.

She's safe with us.

We enter the men's bathroom on the south side of the school. Luca is here with the two cheerleaders bent over the sinks, palming the counter. Their legs are spread, and from across the room, I can see their pussies are glistening with cum.

Alex gasps when she sees the girls. She doesn't know Luca the way we do. He's spiteful, mean, and a vindictive son of a bitch. Using us to get back at him was the wrong move. Because if she really wants him, he'll never let her forget this mistake.

It's another strike against her.

He already hates her because of her family. Just hearing the last name Wellington sets Luca off the deep end. For years, he dreamed of how he would make them pay. But Carl is a Founder and untouchable.

So Alex will have to do.

Luca unbuckles his belt and hooks it around Stacey's neck while staring at Alex in the mirror. He's going to fuck both of them and make her watch. And if she tries to run, Bash and I will stop her.

Luca removes a condom from his pocket and rolls it down his length. Alex looks at me, then Bash, waiting for one of us to stop him.

We can't.

She doesn't understand that these girls mean less than nothing to Luca. He uses their bodies, and that's it. I've never heard him speak to them other than to bark an order. They don't know him and never will. Luca doesn't let anyone get close to him.

No one but us.

He's never even kissed a woman. Well, neither have I, but I have my reasons. And so does Luca. We both hate being touched and can't stand intimacy. Bash is my exception, but Luca doesn't have one.

Or does he?

The way he stares at Alex while he fucks Stacey says more than words. She could be Luca's exception.

Alex leans back against the wall between us and grabs our hands. "Fuck him," she whispers as Luca pulls out and sinks his dick back into Stacey with his eyes on Alex. "I want both of you. Touch me." She drags our hands up higher. "Make me come. He can fuck all the whores he wants, but he'll never have me."

I see Luca's nostrils flare in the mirror. He's listening to everything she says and looks like he wants to snap her neck. Only Luca can still look mean as shit while he's getting his dick wet. This crazy motherfucker is worse than me with his anger issues.

I lift her leg over the top of mine and spread her legs for Bash and Luca to get a good look. Luca's jaw tightens, his sole focus on Alex. He doesn't even see the girl in front of him.

Bash grabs his dick over his pants, licking his lips. "Mmm, Cherry. Your pussy is perfect." He leans into her, pressing his nose against her cheek. "I will devour you when the time comes to ditch your pesky virginity."

"I love how you think you're getting my virginity." She smirks, guiding his hand between her legs, pushing one of his fingers between her wet folds. "Bash," she moans, keeping her gaze on Luca, holding his wrist while he pumps his finger into her. "Oh, God."

She's extra loud to gain Luca's attention, which she's had the entire time. He can't stop looking at her in the mirror, gaining pleasure from her screams.

Luca's eyes are wild with anger. He pulls out of Stacey without coming and moves on to the next girl. Stacey tries to complain, and he covers her mouth with his hand.

"Shut up or get out."

He's annoyed he can't get off with the head cheerleader. And if a hot chick like Stacey doesn't do it for him, I doubt he'll come inside Carrie. He wants to fuck Alex but won't let himself stop hating her.

This pisses off Alex even more. And to my surprise, she turns to me and unzips my pants.

I put my hand over hers. "What are you doing, Pet?"

"I'm going to make you come." She licks her lips. "You good with that?"

Our little virgin isn't as sweet as she looks. For a girl who's never been kissed, she's becoming bold. I think Luca has a lot to do with that. For whatever stupid reason, she wants him. Every time he touches another girl, she's seething mad and soaking through her panties.

I drop her leg and whip out my dick, letting her take the lead. "Do you know what to do with it, Pet?"

She chuckles. "I think I can figure it out."

Her tiny hand wraps around my shaft, and she gives me a few pumps, looking up at me to see if she's doing it right. My eyes close for a second, and when they open again, I'm staring at Alex and Bash as his thumb circles over her clit.

He raises Alex's leg to change the angle while she's working my dick. She's going too slow for my taste, forcing me to help. It's her first time touching a dick, and she doesn't know what to do with it.

My hand covers hers, and her eyes light up, breathing harder as she approaches the finish line. Now that she's applying the right amount of pressure, I may come.

Alex has forgotten about Luca, even though he's doing everything to regain her attention. Slapping Carrie's ass. Yanking on her hair. Making the girls kiss and touch each other.

Bash and I are used to Luca's antics. We're not phased and don't bother diverting our gazes from Alex. She's all we care about, anyway. I know she's the key to there being an *us* one day.

Alex.

Bash.

And me.

She's coming on Bastian's fingers, and I feel the intense pressure build in my balls. I'm so close, tightening my grip on her hand, needing her to be as rough as Bastian. Women never go hard enough with me. They think they're going to break my dick. But the pain is what does it for me. Pleasure and pain are the same fucking thing.

Alex comes, a tremor rocking through her body, and seconds later, my cum shoots all over her hand. She's breathing so hard that it takes a moment for her chest to stop rising and falling rapidly.

Bastian raises his fingers to his mouth and sucks her juices from them. She watches, and then her eyes flick back to Luca.

He still hasn't come, taking turns with the girls who do nothing for him. If I were Luca, I would call it a day. Alex is the only woman he wants to fuck. And until he admits that to himself, he will be walking around with blue balls and that miserable fucking expression on his face.

Alex stares at Luca in the mirror and lifts her hand, flipping him the middle finger. And then she proceeds to suck my cum from her skin, licking it clean while she tells him to go fuck himself.

Bastian laughs. "Aww, shit, Cherry. You're going to pay for that later."

"What's he gonna do about it?" Alex moves to the sink beside Stacey and washes her hands, smirking at Luca, acting like he's not mid-fuck with some whore. "You can fuck every girl at this school, Luca. In fact, I hope you do. My grandfather is giving me a choice between you and your brothers. And when I'm forced to choose, it won't be you."

Teeth gritted, he pulls out of Carrie, his cock so big it could be used as a weapon. "Get the fuck out." She doesn't move until he slaps her ass. "I'm talking to you, bitch. Go!" He looks at Stacey. "You, too." He tips his head at the door. "Now!"

"What the fuck, Luca?" Stacey complains, fixing her skirt back into place. "You're ditching us for her?"

"You have three seconds." He rips off the condom and throws it in the trash, tucking his dick back into his pants. "If you don't leave now, I will drag you out by your hair."

That's all it takes for the girls to scramble out of the room and dart into the hallway, giggling.

Luca hovers over Alex as she towel dries her hands. "When the time comes, baby girl, you'll beg me to fuck you."

Blonde curls fall in front of her eyes with each shake of her head. "Not a chance."

He backs her into the counter until she's bent backward over the sink. She grips the edges of the porcelain to sit up. But Luca moves between her legs and slides his hand up her stomach. His fingers graze her tits, continuing his slow exploration before he chokes her.

"Luca," she mutters, eyes wide, excited having him this close. "What are you doing?"

His lips nearly touch hers. "You. Are. Mine." He reaches between them with his free hand and grabs her pussy. "This is mine, too. Remember that the next time you think about playing fucking games with me, Drea."

She narrows her eyes at him. "Drea?"

He doesn't answer.

Until now, he's never called her that. Luca doesn't give people nicknames.

Interesting.

"You want me, Luca?" Alex puts her hands on his chest, which I expect him to swat away, but he doesn't. "Then stop fucking cheerleaders in front of me. No more blowjobs. No more bullshit. If you start treating me right, maybe you can have me one day."

The bell sounds in the hallway. It's the end of lunch, and Luca won't let Alex be late for class. He's pulling too many strings to get her into RISD and needs her to maintain her GPA.

Luca steps out from between her legs and grabs her hand like a rotten child he wants to punish, leading her toward the door. He looks at Bash and me, nods, and then we follow him into the hallway.

Something has changed. And I'm not sure if it's for the better.

Chapter Nine

It's Friday night. Our football team is playing a rival prep school for the championship. And since Marcello is the quarterback, we must support our baby bro.

We stop by the locker room before the start of the game. Marcello waits by the entrance, dressed in his uniform sans helmet.

I watch as Alex notices him and licks her lips. She's into all four of us and doesn't hide it.

Not even from Luca.

Since *that* day in the bathroom, Luca hasn't fucked another cheerleader in front of Alex. No more blowjobs in the cafeteria. He doesn't touch a single girl at Astor Prep.

Life gets easier for Alex.

With all of us watching over her, she's more protected than anyone in Devil's Creek, preserved like the rare art in our home.

She's untouchable.

Luca respects her for standing up to him. I thought he would push back and make her life miserable. Instead, he puts Alex between the three of us when we walk her to class. He keeps her at his right side, where Bash used to be.

One day she will be the Queen of The Devil's Knights. But my hope of her being ours dwindles each day he shows

She's his exception.

But she's still ours until he lays down the law and claims Alex for himself.

Bash pats Marcello on the arm. "Good luck, brother."

I nod when he looks at me. We don't speak much, and I'm not a big talker, anyway.

Alex steps forward, wearing a blue and white Astor Prep football jersey that stops above her belly button. She's got it tied in the back, showing off a decent amount of skin.

Luca offered her the jersey because she wanted to show her school spirit. I also think he gave it to her just to see how our last name will look on her.

He only wore the jersey for freshman year. Luca said football was stupid. But the truth was Luca wanted to cut classes and sit on the bleachers, smoking weed and pissing off teachers. Football wasn't worth his time, even though he was good at it.

The jersey says SALVATORE on the back. And when Alex stands on her tippy toes and hugs Marcello, he leans over to look at her back, giving Luca a curious look.

Luca shrugs.

"Good luck, Marcello." Alex tightens her grip around his neck and kisses his cheek, leaving a red lipstick kiss behind.

He lifts her feet off the ground, grabbing a handful of her ass, which looks amazing in black yoga pants that hug her in all the right places. And now that she's gaining some weight, her body is filling out. Even her tits are getting bigger. They've got to be closer to a D cup.

He hugs her back, staring over her shoulder at Luca. "Thanks, princess."

Marcello enjoys provoking Luca. Showing Alex this much affection pisses him off. He balls his hands into fists at his sides and glares at his brother.

They have never been close. Not even as kids. And Marcello rarely talks to Bash and me. He doesn't trust us, even though we have been his brother for ten years. But his distrust mostly comes from his ill feelings toward Luca.

Alex wets her finger and dabs at the lipstick on Marcello's cheek. "Oops! Sorry about that." She rubs at the same spot until it's gone. "I don't want your teammates giving you shit."

He rolls his broad shoulders. "I don't care. Maybe it will be good luck."

Marcello is a year and a half younger than Alex. But you wouldn't know it by looking at him. While Luca is lean and muscular, Marcello is thick in the arms and chest and is built like an athlete.

He's got the arms of a professional boxer, which Alex pays close attention to when she tries to curl her fingers around his bicep and only gets halfway.

She giggles and peeks up at him. "Mmm... Your arms are so big, Marcello."

He bends down and whispers, "My arms are not the only big thing on my body." He winks, and she blushes ten shades of red. "I'm going to win this game for you, princess."

"Yeah?" Alex clings to his side. "I'll be in the stands cheering for you."

Alex gives him one more kiss on his cheek, and he kisses her back.

"Break a leg," Luca tells his younger brother.

His words almost sound like he wants him to break a leg because he's jealous of Alex's reaction to him. He can't stand any competition.

So why did he ever ask us to fuck with her? It was his idea for us to reenact his fantasies while he watched.

Luca plans for everything but didn't expect to like her. His feelings for Alex have put a wrench in his strategy. Letting the three of us get closer to her was a mistake on his part.

He knows it now.

"Cello," Sonny Cormac calls out to Marcello as he pops

out of the locker room. "Yo, we're up in five. Stop fucking around."

Marcello and Sonny have been best friends since birth. He doesn't have Luca or us, so he spends most of his time with Sonny and Drake Battle when he's home from MIT. Drake is a genius, so even though he should be in the same grade as Marcello, he's already in college.

"Well, what do we have here?" Sonny shoves a hand through his short, blond hair, glancing at Alex. "Little Wellington. Did you come to wish us luck?"

"Of course." She beams a smile at him. "Good luck, Sonny."

Sonny scoops her into his arms and gives her a good squeeze. "Thanks, beautiful." He glances at Luca first, then at Bastian and me. "Are these animals taking good care of you?"

"Mind your business, Cormac," Luca snaps, tugging Alex away from Sonny. "Better get your ass on the field. Don't want to be late, golden boy."

Sonny snorts with laughter. "Fuck off."

Marcello takes one last look at Alex, smiles, and then heads into the locker room with Sonny.

"If you touch my brother like that again," Luca snaps at Alex, "we're going to have a fucking problem, Drea."

She folds her arms under big tits and scowls. "I hugged Marcello, you crazed lunatic. Is hugging not allowed in the Luca Salvatore rulebook?"

Bastian laughs. "Cherry, you know better than to poke the dragon. Remember what he did the last time?"

Alex tugs at the long hair slung over her shoulder. "Oh, like fuck those cheerleaders while I watched?" Then, aiming her eyes at Luca, she says, "You do that shit to me again, and I'll make you watch me fuck every player on the football team —including Marcello."

"Go ahead, baby girl." Luca gets in her face, his top lip quivering with anger he can't hide. "See if I care."

She pushes her hands to her hips, facing off with him. "How about I start with Bash and Damian?"

He holds up his hands and shrugs. "If that's what you want."

With that, Alex yanks on my belt and starts ripping it off like she's possessed. "You wanna get your dick sucked while Luca watches, Damian?" Then her eyes flick to Bastian. "How about you, Bash? I think I can handle you both."

"Cherry," Bash groans and unzips his pants. "You sure you wanna do this?"

Her expression says no, but she's so mad at Luca that I bet she would do anything right now.

Luca moves behind her, his hand sliding up her stomach and dipping beneath the jersey. "Do you even know how to suck a dick, baby girl?" His nose smashes into her cheek. "Huh? Think you can handle all three of us? Because my cock is much bigger than my brothers. And I doubt you could fit half of me in your smart-ass mouth."

She rolls her eyes. "Your whores don't seem to have a problem."

"Those sluts lost their virginity in seventh grade," he spits back. "But you're not like them, Drea. You're a good girl. And when the time comes, you're going to be really fucking bad for us."

"What happened to not being allowed to hug your brothers?"

"You can touch Bash and Damian."

Her eyes narrow at him. "But not Marcello?"

Luca nods.

"Why are you jealous of Marcello?"

His hands fall from her body, and he takes a step back. "I'm not. Marcello is not like us. Just leave it alone, Drea."

"No," she challenges, turning around to face him. "Why is Marcello the exception to your fucked up rules? Is it because he's the only nice Salvatore brother?"

"I'm nice to you," Bash interjects.

"Yeah, but you're also kind of an asshole sometimes." She looks at me. "And Damian has more mood swings than Luca."

"Get used to us, Cherry." Bastian curls her tiny body into his, running his hand over her ass. "You're stuck with us for life."

She laughs. "For life?"

I clutch her chin, forcing her eyes to meet mine. "Yes, Pet. For life. Til' death do us fucking part."

Chapter Ten

THE LIBRARY IS TOO QUIET. IF I'M LEFT ALONE FOR TOO LONG with my thoughts, the darkness always seems to settle into my body and suffocate me. I don't like having disgusting urges. It's sick of me to stare at Alex and wonder how her blood will taste.

I know that.

But I'm curious and want to know everything about her. Will she scream if I take out my hunting knife and cut her inner thigh? Just a little slice, only enough to draw blood. I wonder if she'll whimper if I bend down and lick the blood from her skin. Or will she soak through her panties like she does when Luca yells at her?

These are the kind of thoughts I struggle with daily. Bash has already warned me not to show Alex my true nature. He's afraid I will scare her away.

Alex sits between Bash and me, reading from the textbook on the table in front of her. She twirls her finger around a long, blonde curl, lost in her thoughts. Her beauty startles me, making me want to mess her up, so she's not so fucking perfect.

Bash likes that she's untainted. He gets off knowing we'll be the only men ever to touch her. When she first arrived in Devil's Creek, she was innocent but never sweet.

I like when she's bad.

There's a dark side to Alex Wellington she hides beneath

her gorgeous surface. On the outside, she looks like an heiress. Beautiful. Manicured. But make no mistake, our girl is wild, begging to be free.

Alex's head snaps to me as if she can feel me watching her. A smile curls up the corners of her mouth. "What are you looking at?"

Invading her personal space, I lean forward so our elbows touch on the table. "You."

"Yeah?" Her blue eyes light up. "Do I have something on my face? You keep looking at me like I do."

I shake my head.

She slides her chair closer until our thighs brush under the table. Her hand rests on my leg, too close to my cock that's growing harder with each second. "You stare at me a lot when you don't think I notice."

I shrug, seeing no point in denying the truth. "So? You got a problem with it, Pet?"

She smiles. "I'm not a pet, Damian."

I grab her hand that keeps running up and down my leg and hold it over my cock. "Feel this, Pet?"

She nods, licking her lips.

Clutching her wrist, I guide her hand, and she rubs my dick over the top of my pants. "This is what you do to me."

Bash leans over Alex, staring at me with a smirk plastered on his face. "Ooh, I want to play."

She has no idea what he really means. When the time comes, she'll learn all about our relationship. Alex will be taking both of our cocks at the same time. And if my brothers get their way, she'll be fucking all four of us.

"Then play with us," Alex coos, licking her glossy red lips as she unzips my pants.

How did we get this lucky?

When we first learned of the big pharma princess, we thought she'd be a stuck-up bitch. But not Alex. She's been down to earth from the start and easy for us to mold.

Easy to train.

She takes orders well and doesn't give us shit now that she knows what to expect.

Bastian hikes up her skirt high enough for me to see the new panties I bought her. All week, I have ripped off a pair each day, only to reward her with new ones.

She likes this game.

I do, too.

"See through," Bash says with a wicked smirk, taking a good look at the black lace that leaves zero to the imagination. "Mmm... Cherry, you're already wet for us." He pushes the fabric inside her and whispers, "Your pussy is begging to be fucked."

A soft moan slips past her lips. "Bash." Her eyes drift to me when he thrusts inside her again. "Damian."

I love the way she says my name.

But before we can get started, the bell rings.

Stupid fucking bell.

"To be continued, Cherry." Bash licks the cum from his fingers and kisses her cheek. "We can play while we eat lunch."

OF COURSE, LUCA MESSES UP OUR PLANS. HE YANKS ALEX onto his lap, curling his arm around her with possession. He's been acting strangely for weeks. Whenever Bash or I touch her, he steals her away.

The tension between the three of us is thicker than syrup. While he hasn't outright said anything, Luca claims Alex for himself, fucking up the deal we made.

She cozies up on his lap and leans into his chest, rubbing his public display of affection in Stacey and Carrie's faces. I don't even think Alex likes Luca. But when the cheerleaders snap their heads at them, green with envy, Alex flicks her hair over her shoulder and smiles.

"Keep grinding on my dick like that, baby girl," Luca growls in her ear, digging his fingers into her thigh. "I will bend you over this table and tear your hymen to shreds."

"Luca." She gasps. "No, you won't."

His hand slides up her leg, inching beneath her skirt. "Yes. I. Will." He bites out each word, speaking slowly but with heat behind each word. "Don't fucking test me, woman. I'll break the deal I made with my brothers to spite you."

Alex narrows her eyes at him. "What deal?"

"Not your concern." He shakes his head and lifts her off his lap. "Go sit with my brothers."

She glances across the table at Bash and me for answers.

Neither of us responds.

Bastian stuffs a slice of pizza into his mouth and ignores her question. I shrug, leaving her to wonder what tricks we have up our sleeves.

The suspense is killing her.

Alex drops into the chair beside me, placing her hand on my knee. "So, what are you three hiding from me?"

"Nothing," I lie.

She doesn't need to know we have no intention of making her choose which of us she will marry. Because once she gets a taste for us, she won't want to let any of us go.

That's always been the plan. But Luca's changed his mind about her.

Well, sort of.

He's still lukewarm about marrying Alex. Despite his recent actions, he still hates her family. No amount of time will change that. But he's coming around to the idea of having her in his life.

Besides, our father will kill Luca if he screws this up for

our family. They need this marriage and can't afford to let her slip through their fingers over a feud.

Arlo thought he could adopt Bastian and me as a favor to Bastian's grandfather. But that plan backfired. Fitzgerald Archibald Adams IV never intended to let the Salvatores into The Founders Society. Marriage is the only way, and so is having an heir with Founders' blood.

Alex stares at me, mentally probing me for answers. But I'm not telling her shit. If Luca wants her to know, he will tell her. We don't break the deals we make with each other, regardless of what he said to her.

I hook my arm around her and pull her onto my lap. Our little virgin is always horny and easily distracted. So I reach under her skirt, skimming the hem of her panties.

Today, she's wearing black lace that feels amazing on my fingertips. And she smells sweet, like sugar and sex.

"Damian." She swats at my hand. "What are you doing? People are right there."

"Hasn't stopped us before." I tilt her head back and suck on her neck as I shove her panties to the side. "Do you want to come, Pet?"

She no longer cares about what anyone at this school thinks and nods. "Oh, God," she moans when my fingers breach her wet folds. As usual, she's dripping for us. "Yes."

No one pays any mind to us. They act like we're not here, all while watching us out of the corners of their eyes. But she doesn't know that.

Our girl hasn't attended Astor Prep long enough to know we always have the attention of everyone in the room. It comes with being a Salvatore.

Bastian grips her thigh, spreading her legs wider for him to see how wet she is for us. "Look at my sweet Cherry. Baby, you're dripping on Damian's hand." His eyes dart across the table to Luca. "Your pussy gets wetter the meaner Luca is to you. Isn't that right?"

She leans back against my chest, clutching my thighs, and moans.

"Squeeze my fingers, Pet." I suck on her earlobe and shove another finger inside her tight pussy. "I'm not stopping until your cum soaks my pants."

"Damian," she whispers, riding my hand like a good girl.

Luca slides his chair closer, resting his elbows on the table, staring at Alex like a hunter. He could have easily torn her apart at the seams, making her beg for more. But he refuses to go farther than what he's done with her. The little bit of touching is already too much for Luca.

I glance at the tables surrounding us. We're all clear to our right and behind Luca, but the students to my left are starting to notice what's happening over here.

I tip my head, gesturing at Luca for him to deal with the nosy bastards. He nods and gets out of his chair. All it takes is my brother shooting a menacing glare at the assholes spying on us.

They want an invite to our not-so-private show. I don't care who listens, but no one without the last name Salvatore is laying their eyes on our woman.

People whisper about us, same as usual. It gets old being the center of attention. The family everyone in Devil's Creek talks about. They gossip about us because we keep our secrets guarded. Only the founders of the town know anything real about us.

Bastian leans over my leg and circles Alex's clit with his thumb. "You're so close, Cherry." He slides one finger in beside mine, and she whimpers, forcing him to cover her mouth with his hand. "If we pull out our fingers, is your pussy going to gush all over Damian's pants?"

She can't answer with his hand over her mouth. So she rocks her hips into our hands and nods, her body trembling as an orgasm rips through her.

Luca scoots his chair closer to us, blocking Alex from the

view of onlookers. He looks like he's seconds from losing his cool, hand curled into a fist on the table. His jaw flexes with each moan that falls from Alex's lips.

We're all obsessed with her—even Luca. Our brother will never admit he has feelings—let alone feelings for *her*—but he wants her.

I look at Bastian, who's wearing a Joker-like grin, removing his finger from her sweet pussy at the same time as mine. Our eyes dip between Alex's thighs.

Cum drips out of her, sliding down her thighs and onto my pants. Just a few drops. But it's enough to satisfy the sick need inside me.

I want to walk around the school for the rest of the day knowing I did this to her. Proof that she wants me and this could work between us. Her body craves me, but I need more than her body to keep her and Bash.

This will have to do for now.

It's a good start.

I raise my finger to my mouth and suck, licking every bit of her cum from my skin. If Bastian didn't worry about bringing shame to our family, I'd let him lick her cum from my finger. He would if we were alone. But around outsiders, he will never lower his guard. We already have enough people talking shit about our family.

So he licks the finger he had inside her. *I wish my finger was your cock*, his gray eyes say with each flick of his tongue.

Alex doesn't know about our dirty little secret. She knows the two of us are close but hasn't a clue that our brotherly bond is anything but brotherly.

We have been best friends our entire lives, from the moment our mothers brought us into this world. Our parents even gave us similar-sounding names, knowing we were destined for each other.

Bastian.

Damian.

People think we're blood brothers because of our names. They don't know that we were once different people and lived another life.

The bell rings over the loudspeakers. The room breaks out into a cacophony of voices. People shout and exit the cafeteria.

Alex hops up from my lap, fixing her skirt into place. She glances at me. "I have to stop by the bathroom." Her gaze lowers to the cum on my pants. "You should, too."

"Nah." I rise from the chair, sliding my hand onto her hip. "I want the reminder of you."

Luca raises his hand and beckons Alex with his index finger. He doesn't need to put his hands on her to gain her attention. Just being in the same airspace, she gravitates toward him. Their natural chemistry is unbelievable, and yet he doesn't see it.

He's too blinded by his hatred for her family to notice what's right in front of him. She would be *his* in a heartbeat. All he would have to do is say the word.

Chapter Eleven

THE REST OF THE SCHOOL YEAR DOESN'T GO AS PLANNED. Luca finally takes his head out of his ass and realizes he's losing Alex to us. His jealousy is taking a nasty turn, making him even more insufferable than usual.

At home, he barks orders, treating us like children instead of his brothers. He hasn't spoken to Marcello in over a month and refuses to acknowledge him. Jealousy is not a good look on Luca.

Luca slams my locker shut, jaw set hard, his menacing blue eyes fixed on me. "No more, Damian." His gaze flicks to Bastian with the same intense expression crossing his face like a dark storm cloud. "You, too, Bash. She's *mine*."

There he goes with that word again. Lately, Luca has been saying Alex is his when she was ours from the start. That was part of the deal we made before she arrived in Devil's Creek.

Alex is in the bathroom, changing into a different pair of panties because I ripped them off her. I think she likes our little game. She never knows what I'll make her wear or when I will steal her panties.

Little does she know I'm addicted to her smell. I lose my fucking mind every night when I get home, dreaming of how she will feel when I fuck her.

"No more what, brother?" Bastian asks, rolling his eyes. "You're going to have to use your words if you're trying to make a point."

"My point," Luca snaps, "is that Alex is mine. And I don't want either of you touching her anymore."

Bastian bares his teeth, snarling at Luca. "Fuck you. Since when do you give a shit about her?"

"I don't," he lies. "But I don't trust either of you not to fuck her. We have a deal, and you're getting really fucking close to breaking it."

Luca won't fuck Alex, even though he wants her. And if the prick can't have her, then no one can. He's always been like this. A damn baby when he doesn't get his way.

"We keep our promises," I interject, not liking his tone or how he speaks to us like idiots. "We won't fuck Alex. Neither will Marcello."

Alex saunters toward us. Blonde curls brush the tops of her breasts, which are getting bigger. She's eating meals with us at school and filling out nicely, her curvy body made for sin.

Made for *us*.

Luca curls his arm around her, pressing her back into his chest. She relaxes in his arms and peeks up at him, a smile on her lips.

Every girl at Astor Prep craves the same attention from Luca. He's the most popular person at this school and has the eye of every woman in a ten-mile radius.

Women look at me the same way. But they're usually smart enough to steer clear of me. They know my good looks mask the sinister parts of my soul. And while Luca is intimidating, he's not frightening.

Not like me.

"You're coming with me today after school, Drea." Luca dips his head down, his nose brushing her cheek. "I'm taking you to an art gallery in Manhattan."

"What?" Alex's eyes widen, and she spins around to face him. "Are you serious?"

He nods, keeping his gaze on Bash and me, and winks. "I

want to introduce you to a friend of my mother's. She can help with your art career."

"Wow," she mouths, fanning herself with her hand. "Who are we meeting?"

"Arianna Lacoste."

"Oh, my God. I love her work." She throws her arms around his neck and kisses his cheek. "Thank you, Luca."

I notice him stiffen at her closeness, but he doesn't push her way. My brother actually puts his hand on her back. He hates human contact as much as me. So it's weird seeing him hugging Alex.

She's *his* exception.

I can't fuck this up for him. Not when I already have my exception. If anyone ever took Bastian from me, I would gut them like a fish and drink their fucking blood.

Luca grips Alex's ass and lifts her feet off the ground, rubbing this rare moment of affection in our faces. His body is pressed against hers, but his attention is on us. He's taking her away from us because he can. And because he knows we won't fight him.

We never do.

Bastian is the only one who ever challenges Luca. And with something this important to our family, we won't interfere. In the end, Luca or Marcello has to marry her. And it might as well be Luca.

I hold up my hands, gesturing that I'll back off. Luca snaps his head at Bash, waiting for his nonverbal response.

He nods.

We owe everything we have and everything we have become to the Salvatores. They took us into their home when we were scared little boys with no parents and nowhere to go. So even though it kills both of us to let Alex go, we don't have a choice.

He wants her.

And she's his.

Chapter Twelve

I WAKE UP IN THE DARK, STARING AT THE BLACK WALLS OF MY bedroom, heart pounding in my chest. Another nightmare. The dreams have worsened since the day Luca claimed Alex.

Every time, I lose Bastian.

That's my worst nightmare, the one thing I dread more than anything. He's been distant and won't let me touch him. Our dynamic is off, and I know it's because of Alex.

We still see her at school. But Luca keeps her at his side like a dog. Sometimes, he puts her on his knee and strokes her hair to piss us off. She thinks he's being sweet and melts into his arms. Alex doesn't know he's only being nice to fuck with our heads.

To fuck with *hers*.

Drenched in sweat, I sit up and slide my legs off the side of the mattress. Running a hand through my black, damp hair, I brush the longer strands off my forehead. My skin is hot and sticky, and for a moment, it still feels like I've lost Bastian.

The dream *feels* too real.

In my mind, I see his blood on the cold, stone floor. His neck snapped, head turned to the side. I don't know where we are—maybe on Skull Island for The Devil's Knights initiation.

Our dad says it will be the hardest two months of our lives. He says we will bleed and hurt and wish we are dead

I can't lose Bastian.

And yet, I am.

He's pulling away.

I creep out of my bedroom in the middle of the night, desperate to see Bastian, needing to know he's okay. That he's still breathing.

Slipping inside his room, I close the door and get in bed with him. Bash is curled up on his right side, cradling the pillow with his lips parted. In sleep, he looks peaceful. I watch his chest rise and fall, blowing out a relieved breath that he's alive.

He's safe.

I roll onto my side to face him and grab his hand, threading my fingers between his. The sudden movement causes him to rock into me, tightening his grip on my hand. A tiny smile turns up the corners of his mouth.

I brush the messy, brown hair off his forehead and kiss his skin. It's been a while since I felt this close to him. Bastian is the only person who understands me inside and out. We don't have any secrets.

Bash rests his head on my shoulder. "Can't sleep, D?"

"No. I had another nightmare."

He squeezes my fingers. "What was it this time?"

"You were dead," I choke out, sickened by the memory of him lying dead on the ground and unable to help him. "I think I killed you on accident."

"One day, you probably will," he says in a sleepy tone, one eye open. "We have to get your urges under control."

"I've been on my best behavior." I lean forward, our faces only inches apart, and stare at his lips. "But I have to do something for Dad this weekend."

Bastian scowls. "I'm going with you. Just in case."

He doesn't like what I become when I have to kill our family's enemies. Hell, I don't like it, either. I don't want to be wired this way.

It's a compulsion.

People with OCD must consistently check the lock on their front door until it drives them insane.

I have to kill.

Thankfully, I don't feel the sudden need all the time. It comes and goes, but I turn into a different person when the switch flips.

I'm not myself.

I'm a monster.

Bash turns onto his back, pulling his hand away from mine. "You've been better, I'll give you that. But you haven't been doing so hot since Luca took Alex away."

"Neither have you," I shoot back. "We don't even fuck around anymore. It's like you're sickened by me."

"Never," he says without hesitation. "You know damn well how I feel about you, Damian. So don't say shit like that."

"You're pissed. So am I."

"Yeah. The. Fuck. I. Am." Bash sits up and reaches into his nightstand, removing a knife from the drawer. He hands it to me. "Do your worst. "

For years, Bash has let me carve into his skin. He has tons of knife wounds that have healed, though some don't look great. The skin is pulled tighter in some places, marring his perfect body.

I take the knife from his hand. "You're in pain, too?"

He nods. "Take it away, D. Just cut my fucking heart out. Because if you don't, watching Luca and Alex will kill me."

She was ours for most of the school year, and now that we're down to the last few weeks, we will lose her again.

I get on top of Bash, pinning him to the mattress. Gliding the knife over his heart, I consider my first incision. He wants me to cut out his heart, but I won't hurt him. Not the way I do my victims.

So I grip the hilt and carve an X over his chest. I take it slow, allowing him to adapt to the pain. Bastian is letting me permanently mark his skin because he trusts me. He knows I will never hurt him.

Blood drips down his chest, and I bend forward to taste him. My entire body trembles as the need takes over. The hunger inside me blooms, and the familiar metallic scent fills the room.

My cock hardens as I taste his blood, getting a hint of saltiness from his skin. I rub against his inner thigh to create some friction, desperate for a release. He's hard too and pokes my stomach with his length.

I want to consume him.

Be one with him.

Even though I can't control my urges, I only have to see his face or hear his voice to come back to reality.

"Damian." I look up as his eyes slam shut, and he bites his bottom lip. "I hate feeling like this," he says through clenched teeth. "I fucking hate *him.*"

"I know, B." I dab at the blood sliding down his chest and lick it from my finger. "But Luca is our brother. He's family. And our family needs us to forget about her. It's the right thing to do."

I'm rarely the coherent one. Bash usually tells me what we need to do, not the other way around. But he's struggling with not having Alex anymore. He was looking forward to there being an us someday.

I was, too.

Disappointment crashes into my chest as I bend down and flatten my tongue over his skin again. Whenever I need a release, Bash lets me do this. I've tasted his blood dozens of times and never get enough of him.

His fingers slip through my hair. "Damian," he whispers. "Look at me."

I lift my head until our eyes meet.

"I think I'm in love with her."

My heart nearly stops at his confession. He's known her for months, but still... Bastian can't love her.

Anger furrows my brows, and I'm thankful it's dark in his room, so he can't see my reaction. A part of me has always been jealous of what Bash has with Alex.

He's not afraid to express his feelings toward her in public. They're not lurking in the shadows, hiding their dirty deeds from the world.

"What does love feel like?" I ask because I have no idea.

He rips the hunting knife from my hand and drops it onto the bed. "It feels like... The way I feel about you but different."

"How is it different?" I slide off him, annoyed. "Because she's a woman, and that makes everything right in your head?"

"No," he growls. "Fuck, Damian. What is your problem?" Bash leans back against a stack of pillows, blood dripping from his wound and sliding down his stomach. "I don't have different feelings for you because you're a man. That doesn't matter."

"Yes, it does," I challenge. "It matters. Public perception is important to you."

"We have to protect our family," he fires back. "If The Founders ever found out about us, they would never let our dad and brothers into The Society. You know that. So fuck..." He tugs at the ends of his hair. "Stop giving me shit about it."

"Sorry," I blurt out, but I don't mean it.

"Luca will never love her." He scrubs a hand across his jaw and sighs. "And I hate that he gets to keep her."

I move beside him, shoving a pillow behind me to prop myself against the headboard. "What are you gonna do about it?"

He shrugs. "What can I do? After everything Dad has done for us, I can't fuck up his chances of getting into The Founders Society. Alex is their only option."

"We'll always have each other." I put my hand over the top of his on the mattress. "I'm not going anywhere."

"I know, D. Don't worry." His head snaps to me. "I'm not leaving you either. But I need some time to decompress. Luca's got my head all fucked up over her."

"I can kill him," I suggest as a possible solution to our problem.

He laughs, thinking I'm kidding. Luca is my brother, but Bash is my everything. I'd do anything for him. And I don't like seeing him upset or hurt.

"I doubt Luca would be that easy to kill. That mother-fucker is a demon straight out of Hell. Thanks for the offer, though."

I lay back on a pillow, and Bash curls up beside me. He throws his arm over my stomach and breathes on my neck. "I can't give you everything you want. Not now, anyway. But you and me? We're forever. Nothing will ever change that. It's always been us against the world."

Chapter Thirteen

ALEX IS SO FUCKING BEAUTIFUL, LYING BENEATH ME WITH A sweet smile on her lips as I shove my cock past her wet folds. I pull out and slam back into her again, fucking her tight pussy until she screams for me. The bedroom smells of sex and sweat, and the only scent we're missing is blood.

I want to taste her.

But I don't get the chance because Bastian is behind me, lubing my asshole with his finger. My cock twitches inside her. If Bash keeps this shit up, I'm going to explode any second.

"Fuck me, Bash." I reach behind me and grab his shaft. "Don't hold back."

It's finally happening.

This is the moment I have waited years to experience with him. Bastian likes to deny me, but he's wanted this for almost as long as me. It just took him longer to realize it.

A feral grunt rips from my throat when Bash replaces his finger with the tip of his fat cock. He stretches me out good and slowly inches inside me.

It burns, but I'm used to the pain.

I like when it hurts.

Once he's completely inside me, he grunts in my ear, sucking on my skin. "Fuck, Damian. You feel so good."

"See what you've been missing," I toss back at him as I fuck our girl, doing my best to match his rhythm.

He clutches my shoulder and bites down on my skin,

tugging on my flesh hard enough to mark me. I hope he does because I want a visible reminder of him.

His sweat drips onto my back, and with the three of us joined, it's really fucking wet and slippery. Alex moans both of our names, her pussy drenched. A sheen of sweat breaks out across my forehead and brows and slides down my cheek.

"Oh, God, Damian," Alex whimpers, her blue eyes wide as she looks up at me, her big tits bouncing as I fuck her. "Bash," she bites out next. "I love watching you fuck Damian."

"Yeah?" Bastian sounds surprised, though I'm not sure why. "You like getting fucked by two big cocks?"

"Yes," she hisses, her eyes closing as I go deeper.

With each of Bastian's thrusts, I fuck her harder, and her screams of pleasure penetrate the air like gunfire.

I'm so close.

About to come.

And then…

Someone shakes me.

"Damian, wake the fuck up!" Bastian slams his palm down on my arm. "We're going to be late for school."

Breathing hard, I open my eyes and see Bash in the bed beside me. He's hovering over me, already dressed in the Astor Prep uniform.

"What the fuck, Bash? I was having the best dream of my life."

His eyes lower to my cock that's poking through the slit in my boxers and dripping with cum. "Yeah, I can see that." He waggles his eyebrows. "Were you thinking about me?"

"Of course." I sit up and sigh, hating it was a dream. "You fucked me while I fucked Alex. It was so fucking hot."

He bends down and licks the cum from my dick, his eyes on me. "One day, I will. Now get out of bed. You slept through two alarms. Luca wants to get to school early to surprise Alex with something."

I slide my legs off the mattress and rise from the bed. "What kind of surprise?"

He rolls his broad shoulders, which look even larger beneath the academy blazer. "Who knows? Probably something that will piss me off." Bash shakes his head. "I'm so sick of him rubbing Alex in my face. I want to kill him."

"Eventually, he will show her his true colors, and that girl will come running back to us."

He nods in agreement. "It's only a matter of time before he fucks this up."

It's the last week of classes before we graduate. Alex will leave for Providence with her twin brother at the end of the summer. Luca, Bastian, and I will attend Harvard University in the fall.

Cambridge isn't that far from Providence. We'll still keep tabs on her. No way Luca would ever let her out of his sight without having a way to watch her. Our father owns a private security company, so spying on people is one of our specialties.

A few minutes before Alex arrives, Luca shoves a box into Alex's locker. She greets us with a big smile, flicking her blonde curls over her shoulder.

Alex opens her locker and gasps. She pulls out a black box with a pink satin ribbon. "Oh, my God. What is this?"

"Open it," Luca mutters, eyes on the contents of his locker.

I take the box from her and hold it so she can flip off the lid.

"Wow!" Alex's face lights up at the black Valentino dress inside the box. "Which one of you bought this?"

"I did." Luca shuts his locker. "Of course. I'm the only one with any taste in this family."

"Speak for yourself, brother," Bastian snaps, shaking his head at the smug bastard.

The anger practically radiates off Bash. After our talk, I understand why it bothers him so much to see Alex with Luca.

He's in love with her.

Luca shrugs, giving Bastian one of his evil grins. "It's the truth."

Of course, the all-knowing Luca fucking Salvatore thinks he's better than everyone. He has such a chip on his shoulder. The funny thing is Bash and I have a lot more money than our adoptive family.

We made the Forbes Billionaires list as kids after inheriting our parents' airline. So if Luca thinks money makes him better than us, he's so wrong. Once we turn twenty-one and graduate from college, we will inherit the money in our trusts and run Atlantic Airlines together.

Alex looks up at Luca like he's a god. "This is for me?"

"It was in your locker, Drea. Who else would it be for?" Luca's right eyebrow raises a few inches. "Do you like it?"

"Are you kidding?" Alex's cheeks are bright pink, her smile so wide it reaches her big, blue eyes. "I love it."

She hugs Luca, and he looks sickened by having someone touch his skin. He hates it as much as I do. But he doesn't seem to mind when it comes to Alex and grabs her ass, winking at Bash.

I have to grab Bash's arm to keep him from choking Luca. His head snaps at me, teeth clenched. Without speaking, I know what he's thinking. He should have agreed to let me kill Luca. I kinda want to, even though he's my brother. Family. But anyone who hurts Bash deserves my wrath.

"It's beautiful." Alex's arms slip away from Luca's lean but muscular body, a smile plastered on her beautiful face. "But why did you buy this for me? I don't have anywhere to wear it."

He backs her into the locker, his fingers skimming up her right thigh, and smirks. "Because you're *mine*. And I won't have you attending our graduation party without looking like a queen."

She wants him to kiss her.

He won't.

Luca hates intimacy. If anyone even tries to touch his shoulder, he'll snap. It's a side effect of all the abuse. Our father treated him the worst after Eva died. The punishments were severe and painful, reminders of what all of us had lost.

"Luca," she whispers when his lips are inches from hers. "Thank you. It's perfect."

The way she says his name sounds like a girl in love, not a girl who hated him a few months ago. A lot has changed since the day she challenged him.

"You'll wear it on Saturday," he tells her. "And you'll come as my date, understood?"

"Don't tell me what to do, Luca." She's bold and puts her hands on his shoulders, pulling him closer. "You're not the boss of me."

He cups the side of her face with possession. "You are mine, Drea." He presses his forehead against hers in this rare moment of affection. "Say it."

"No," she whispers.

Good for her.

Luca has met his match.

Chapter Fourteen

WE GRADUATED ON FRIDAY FROM ASTOR PREP. AND THE following night, we're forced to attend our graduation party. I could care less about all of this shit. Having too much attention makes me nervous. While Luca likes to be admired, I prefer to be left alone.

Marcello is over by the bar, drinking with his best friend, Sonny Cormac, and the newest addition, Aiden Wellington. They hang out together at school. Luca knows about his friendship with Aiden, even though Marcello thinks he's good at hiding it.

All of them will be Knights one day. But Marcello and Sonny are two years behind us. Aiden graduated with us. However, his stubbornness makes it harder for Carl to talk Aiden into joining The Knights. He's a free spirit like his twin sister and doesn't understand our world.

I find Bastian on the right side of the ballroom, attached to Luca's side. When Bash isn't with me, he's usually with Luca. They're the most alike of the four of us and constantly butt heads. Both of my brothers enjoy the attention and lap it up.

Marcello is like me in some ways. Shy and keeps to himself. He tries to avoid us at all costs. But he's not so bad once he lowers his guard.

I tap Bash on the shoulder. "I'm bored."

"Hmmm..." He turns to look at me, grinning. "I'm sure you can find something to do until the party ends."

I lean into his arm and lower my voice. "I'd like to do you, but you don't touch me anymore."

He scowls, then scans the space around us to ensure no one overheard me. "Damian, for fucks sake. My grandfather is right there. If he hears you..."

Like I don't already know the rules. *What we do in the dark can never see the light.* If anyone were to find out about us, Bastian would be destroyed. He can't handle anyone—especially not his piece of shit grandfather—finding out about us.

Bastian comes from one of the Founding Families. He's an Adams—yes, like the president. Fitzgerald Archibald Adams IV is among the guests in attendance. The old man is one of Bastian's few living relatives and treats him like garbage.

After our parents died, Fitzy took both of us in for a few weeks. Those days of being locked in a dark basement without food or water were worse than hell. Our parents hadn't been in the ground for more than a few days when the beatings started. Some days, we woke up in our piss and shit.

To say we hate Fitzy is an understatement. But he still finds ways to get into Bastian's head. He calls us dirty, filthy animals as if we're still the little boys trapped in the basement, wasting away in the dark.

He's part of the reason I kill people. And why I enjoy hurting bad men who do horrible things and deserve to die. When I kill a man, I imagine it's Fitzy beneath me, begging for his life.

Bastian's grandfather has brainwashed him. He doesn't know about our sexual desires, but he still sees our relationship as wrong. We don't conform to what Fitzy considers the norm. And so Bash sees us as something dirty and disgusting. A secret we need to hide from the world.

"I miss you," I whisper, giving his arm a brotherly pat when I just need an excuse to touch him. No one else will read into the simple gesture. "We leave in the morning for initiation. I *need* to be with you before we go."

There's no time for doing normal post-graduation shit. No senior week or vacation before we start college. Our family isn't like others and has a duty to our corrupt organization.

No rest for the wicked.

"D, it's over." Bastian sips from the highball glass. "Luca is keeping Alex."

"No, I'm not," Luca says, coming out of nowhere with a drink in hand. "You want her? She's yours, too."

"You claimed her, and we've back off since then," Bastian snaps. "And you wait until our last night with her to change your fucking mind?"

Luca smirks. "I'm a dick. What can I say? A little celibacy will do you good with us being locked on Skull Island for the next two months."

All Knights must train on Skull Island before being admitted into the organization. We will go through the nine circles of Hell and hopefully live to tell about it when it's over. Our dad warned us of the dangers will we face.

"What the fuck, Luca?" Bastian's nostrils flare. "You did this shit on purpose." He shakes his head, furious. "The last few months of school were all bullshit, weren't they? A fucking game to mess with our heads."

He shrugs. "I did it more to fuck with *her* head. But sure, if you want to take it personally, go right ahead."

My blood feels like it's boiling inside my veins, and I'm ready to snap my brother's neck.

Luca is a lot of things.

An evil mastermind.

A genius.

And one day, he will lead our family. I respect him, but right now, I want to grab my hunting knife and cut out his black fucking heart.

"You were jealous, weren't you?" I ask him. "That day in

the bathroom set you off, and you haven't been the same with Alex since. You didn't just play her. You played us, too."

"I don't get jealous," Luca fires back with venom in his tone. "But make no mistake, that girl is mine. She will marry me and will produce my heir."

"Yeah," Bastian interjects. "But we had a deal, you jealous fucking prick."

Luca saw how much Alex wanted us, and it killed him. I don't know if Bastian will ever forgive Luca for this. Not sure if I will either… unless he lets us have her and backs off.

"And I intend to keep it." Luca takes a sip from the glass, tugging on his tie. It's red, my favorite color, and it reminds me of blood. "She'll be my wife in name only. You can have her when I'm done. Or if you prefer, we can share her."

I want to kill him.

He made us believe she was off-limits. Neither of us has touched her since. She probably thinks we don't want her anymore when that couldn't be further from the truth.

Bastian sneers at Luca then grabs my arm. "Let's go, D. I need some fucking air."

We exit the ballroom and head toward the back of the house until we reach the veranda that wraps across the back of the property. Dozens of people are sitting at tables, drinking and smoking. I ignore anyone who looks familiar and bolt across the pavers, seeking out the grassy spot at the cliff's edge.

This is where Bash and I go when we need to leave the house. When we first became Salvatores, we felt suffocated all the time. Arlo was always trying to teach us new things.

How to become men. How to handle our finances. How to shoot a gun and how to fight. He even taught me how to kill without getting caught.

My adoptive father understood my dark desires and helped me to embrace them. But there were moments in our childhood when we wanted to run. We wanted to return to Bel Air, where we lived with our parents.

Our parents were laid back and let us do pretty much anything we wanted. But not Arlo. There were rules from day one.

He had schedules for each of us to follow. Specific tasks we had to complete each week. We are better men because of him, but it felt like torture back then.

I'm shocked to find Alex standing at the cliff's edge, the black dress blowing in the wind across the backs of her legs. She's kicked off her heels and standing barefoot in the grass. Her back is to us, long curls draped over her shoulder. Even from behind, she takes my fucking breath away.

I glance at Bastian. He nods, and we each take a side, sandwiching her between us.

Bash leans into her ear. "Are you lost, Cherry?"

She startles at the deep rumble of his voice, throwing her hand over her heart as she turns to look at him. "No. I'm right where I want to be."

His hand slides onto her hip. "What's wrong?"

She studies each of our faces before taking a deep breath. "Luca."

"What did he do?"

"He's acting like his old self." Her eyes leave his and land on the water moving slowly in the bay. "It was all a game to him, I guess."

"That's how he's wired, baby." Bastian pulls her closer. "You'll get used to it."

"I don't want to get used to him." Frown marks line her delicate features. "I hate him. I should have seen right through his lies. He's been too nice to me."

Bastian curls his arm around her, and I watch this rare display of affection. He wants this to work with her. And I need both of them back in my life. I'm sick of not having *them*.

His lips brush hers, and I expect her to step back after not looking at either of us since Luca sank his teeth into her. To her credit, we backed off, thinking this was for the best. That Luca should be with her so our family can get into The Founders Society.

Bastian fists her curls in his palm, parting her lips with his tongue. She opens up for him, their tongues tangling in harmony. It's a sweet kiss at first, but once they get used to each other, Bash is more aggressive. He kisses her the way he sucks my cock. Like he's desperate for more and doesn't want to come up for air.

I'm so fucking jealous.

He rarely kisses women and refuses to kiss me. But maybe this is what he needed for us to get back on track. We only have tonight, and then we won't even think about sex.

On Skull Island, our minds and bodies will be so battered, our father says we'll come home changed. The same men who leave for the island return as someone else. That's the whole point. To train us how to become weapons.

As their mouths separate, Alex is breathing hard.

So is Bash.

He cradles the side of her face and stares into her eyes. "That was some kiss, Cherry."

She smiles. "I'll say."

Alex turns her head to look at me. I can't tell what she's thinking, but her eyes settle on my mouth. Does she want me to kiss her, too?

I'm not ready for that.

I need to fuck her before I think about any other human connection with her. Bash isn't wired like Luca and me. He doesn't get repulsed by the thought of skin-on-skin contact.

He hasn't slept in a grave with a dead body beside him. My brothers don't know the true depths of my darkness. Most of the shit I have done stays with me. I don't share it with anyone, not unless Bastian makes me tell him.

"We leave in the morning." Bastian takes one of her curls

and twirls it around his finger. "And we won't be home until Christmas."

"I'll be in Providence with my brother," she says, her eyes flicking between us. "But Harvard is only an hour's drive from RISD."

"If you don't hit traffic," Bastian adds. "But yeah, it's close. We won't be far away if you need us."

I already know Luca will stalk her from a distance. He's been doing that all year and monitors her cell phone and emails. She will never know the meaning of privacy. Not as long as we are in her life. And she's stuck with us for the fore-seeable future.

Alex grips Bash's tie and pulls him closer, licking her lips. "How about one more kiss? To say goodbye."

"I could kiss you all night, Cherry." He scoops her into his arms and presses his lips to hers. "You're so addicting."

With my hands shoved into my pockets, I stand there and adjust my dick as I watch them. Seeing him happy and turned on by her only makes me want them more.

His lips trace over hers as if trying to savor how she feels. Memorize how she tastes. I want to know, but I won't allow myself. I can't handle another addiction. I already have enough of those.

"We leave in the morning for initiation," Bash tells her as their lips separate.

Alex licks her lips, her blue eyes meeting his gray ones. "Where are you going?"

"A secret location where we'll train to become Knights."

Alex knows our family runs The Devil's Knights. She's also aware that her grandfather is one of the Elders of The Founders Society. But she doesn't fully understand how the two connect and how she fits into the equation. This is the one secret we have been keeping from her. And if her grandfather has explained it to her, she hasn't mentioned it to us.

Bash tucks a blonde curl behind her ear. "I want to see you

again before I leave. It will be a long two months without looking at your pretty face." He leans forward so his lips brush hers. "Two months without doing this."

"Bash," she coos, pressing her palm to his chest.

Her eyes snap to me, and I stand beside them, watching. I don't want a kiss. I have been saving my first kiss for Bash, and until he gives me what I want, I'm not going to cave.

Not even for her.

Chapter Fifteen

I SPENT MOST OF MY CHILDHOOD FEELING LIKE AN OUTSIDER. Even now, I never feel like I belong anywhere. Luca treats me like a child. Marcello ignores me. And my adoptive father acts like I'm a weapon for him to use for his deviant purposes.

But not Bash.

He's the only person who gets me. So as we lay in bed together in our boxer briefs, staring up at the ceiling, I reach for his hand. It feels good to touch him before we go through the most challenging two months of our lives.

"What was it like kissing her?" I ask, purely out of curiosity.

I need to know if I'm missing out. Bash has been smiling all night. He's giddy, which is unusual for him.

"Not the same as other girls I've kissed." A smile is plastered on his face. "She tastes good. You won't believe this." He turns on his side to face me and laughs. "She was wearing cherry-flavored lip gloss."

I laugh. "Weird coincidence."

"Yeah, seriously. It's like it was meant to be." He slides his arm beneath his pillow and looks at me. "I should have kissed her sooner. I'm kicking myself for letting Luca into my head. He fooled both of us."

"Luca only did that so we wouldn't break our promise and take her virginity. He could see she was into us and got all

"She would have given it to us," he says with absolute certainty. "Alex would have been ours if we pursued her. He could see that. Jealous, lying prick."

After Bastian kissed Alex, the three of us went inside. Alex got into a fight with Luca, grabbed her twin, and left our estate. The chances of her showing up tomorrow to see us off before we leave for Skull Island is slim to none.

She was so angry with Luca, tears streaking her cheeks. We didn't hear what he said to her, but whatever it was really upset her. Our brother wouldn't admit what he did. So I left the ballroom with Bash and went straight upstairs to take out our frustrations on each other.

Bastian's lips are inches from mine. I can feel his breath on my skin and wish he would close the distance and kiss me.

He reaches into the nightstand and grabs a black velvet bag and a bottle of lube, dropping them on the bed beside me. "I've got a surprise for you."

I haven't seen Bash this excited in months. It must be because of the kiss. Alex changed his mood instantly, and now I have my best friend back.

Bash removes my gift from the bag, and I stare at him in disbelief.

He got me a dildo.

"It's the same size as my dick." He shoves down his boxers and puts the replica beside his hard cock. "Well, it's the *exact* mold of my dick."

"Why?" I ask him, still stunned by this gesture.

He shrugs. "I'm not ready to give you more. Not yet, anyway. But until then, I want you to know how I will feel inside you."

I narrow my eyes at him. "Until then?"

His words give me hope, and I'm afraid to get too caught up in the moment.

I need this.

I need *him*.

"Yeah," he agrees. "Until I'm ready."

"What if you're never ready?"

He pushes down on my chest and climbs on top of me, his hard cock, digging into my inner thigh. "I will be. Someday."

I run my hands up his chiseled abdomen. "Promise?"

Bash nods. "This is your graduation present." He bends down and kisses my neck, tugging at my flesh with his teeth. "I got this for you months ago, knowing I would surprise you before we leave for initiation. Sorry I've been a dick. I just... I don't know. The thought of us not getting Alex put me in a bad mood. I can see us with her, and I need it to work out."

"It's been fucking torture seeing you withdraw from me when I haven't done anything wrong."

He touches my cheek. "I'm sorry. Let me make it up to you. This is the last time until we get back, okay?"

"Not like we're going to have much alone time on Skull Island with the other recruits."

We'll probably be sleeping on concrete and curling up with a pile of leaves as our pillow. I don't anticipate much sleep on the island.

Bastian starts at my neck, kissing his way down my chest, grinding his cock into my thigh. "I missed this," he whispers between kisses, flicking his tongue over my nipple with his eyes on me. "You make me so fucking hard, Damian."

"I missed you, too," I grunt, lost in the feeling of his hands and tongue on my body.

I don't act the same with him as I do with women. With Bash, I let him take control and pretend to be submissive. It's the only way he will lower his guard and not think too hard about us.

About what this means.

One day, there will be an us, and I can't fucking wait for that day. His gift is the hope I need to get through the next few months. Alex will have years of peace without us. But when it's time to make her our queen, I will finally have what I want.

Him.

Her.

Them.

Bastian licks and bites my skin, teasing me until he drags his tongue up and down my shaft.

"Fuck," I groan, palming the back of his head. "Suck my cock, Bash. Stop teasing me."

He peeks up at me, smiling with his gray eyes as his tongue swirls around the tip. "Only if you beg."

Bash continues to torture me with his long licks, occasionally closing his mouth over the head of my cock, only to pull away.

I press the tip to his lips, on the verge of losing my mind because he's driving me crazy. "Shut the fuck up and take this dick like a good boy before I shove it down your throat."

Laughing, he wraps his hand around the base and gives me a few pumps before he flattens his tongue against my skin, sliding up and down until I'm ready to choke him to death.

I won't.

But God, I want to kill him for fucking with me like this. It's been months of waiting. Months of jerking off to the thought of him. Even when we go to The Mansion, I bend over the girls and take them from behind, using them the way I would Bash.

I grip the ends of his hair and lower his mouth onto me. He looks up at me, holding my gaze as he swallows my cock. Fuck, he looks hot with his cheeks puffed out and spit dripping from his lips. Bash deep-throats me, knowing exactly what I like and the perfect rhythm.

We know each other's bodies better than anyone else. And when he feels the pressure building, he pops my dick out of his mouth and sits up.

"Not yet, D." He grabs the lube from the mattress and

coats his fingers before plunging them into my ass. "I want you to come with my cock in your ass."

It's the closest I'll get to feeling him, and I'm desperate for it. This is the night I have dreamed about for more than two years. I don't care that it will hurt. I hope it does, so I have a reminder of him tomorrow on our ride to the island.

"No more foreplay," I tell him. "Fuck me."

He withdraws his fingers and coats the dildo in lube. The sex toy looks exactly like his dick. It's about nine inches long and thick. So when he inserts the tip into my ass, it stretches me out.

My eyes slam shut from the overwhelming sensations spreading down my thighs. It's the best fucking thing in the world.

Nothing compares to this.

Bash is on top of me, one palm braced on the mattress as he inches the dildo into me. "You okay, D?"

I nod, my eyes snapping open to look at him. "Don't fucking stop, or I'll kill you."

He smirks, inching the dildo the rest of the way, and I block out the initial pain. I've found that when something hurts, I enjoy it more. And as he stares into my eyes, fucking me, I embrace the pain with each thrust.

"One day, I'm going to take Alex's virginity." He slides the toy out and back in as if he were fucking me with the same force. "And then, I'm going to take yours, too."

I don't know if Luca will let him have Alex's virginity. He can sure as hell try. But he can have mine.

It's always been *his*.

With this angle, his dick hits my stomach, so I grab his shaft and stroke it. "I want yours, too." I reach behind him and squeeze his ass. "This is mine."

"Yeah, D," he grunts, thrusting the dildo into me again. "Someday. But we need to work up to that, okay?"

I nod. "I'll wait forever if I have to."

Our conversation ends with us moaning each other's names. I come first, shooting my cum all over his chest, getting some of it on myself. Bash isn't far behind me and adds his cum to what's already on my skin.

He collapses on top of me, the dildo still in my ass and our cum sticking to both of us. "Fuck, that was hot."

I shove my fingers through his hair to push it off his forehead. "This was the best present you've ever given me."

A smile lights up his handsome face. "Yeah?"

I bob my head to confirm.

Bastian rolls off me and removes the dildo. His fingers graze mine as we stare at the ceiling, trying to catch our breaths. We sit silently for five minutes before we're ready to speak again.

"When the timing is right, we'll come for our girl," Bastian says, and it sounds like a promise. "We're not letting her go."

"No, we're not. Luca will never treat her right. She belongs with us."

Chapter Sixteen

As EXPECTED, ALEX DOESN'T COME TO OUR ESTATE TO SEE US
before we leave for initiation. Luca looks bitter about it, but he
doesn't say anything. Though, he doesn't need to. His eyes
keep flicking in the direction of Wellington Manor, which is to
our left as we stand out front with our father.

Bash grits his teeth, eyeing up Luca. He's still mad and has
every right to be. Alex would have shown up if not for our
brother's attitude. Whatever he said to her last night really set
her over the edge.

I brush my fingers against Bastian's, and he glances at me.
We communicate with our eyes, using our unspoken bond. I'm
telling him it's okay to be sad. That I know it fucking hurts. I
know pain better than anyone.

The black limousine parks in the circular driveway. Enzo
gets out and comes around to open the door for us.

"Mr. Salvatore," he says to my dad with a nod, his Italian
accent thick.

Even after all these years, Enzo still sounds like he just got
off the boat from Sicily. He worked for one of the crime
bosses in Italy who gifted him to our family, and he's been
with us ever since.

"Enzo." Dad nods. "It's a big day."

"Yes, sir. Your boys are becoming men." He pats Dad on
the arm. "*Congratulazioni.*"

Luca snorts at his comment, taking offense to being called

a boy. We've been men for years. All three of us look much older than eighteen, and with how we were raised, we're mentally years ahead of our time.

Besides, Luca will be nineteen in July with Bash only a month behind him. And I'm in November.

Marcello stands beside our dad, hands shoved into his jeans pockets. He's wearing a black Henley that makes his huge biceps appear even larger. You can tell he trains daily and never slacks on his workouts.

He's almost seventeen but looks like he's in his twenties. The spitting image of our father, who looked exactly like Marcello and Luca when he was younger. Except his sons are a few inches taller than him.

When the three of them stand side-by-side, I can barely tell them apart. Luca acts exactly like our dad, from how he speaks to the way he moves.

But Marcello is so different from both of them. He's an artist and shy, more like Alex. Marcello doesn't think we know he paints in his room, even though our father forbade it years ago. There is more than what meets the eye with Marcello.

"My boys," Dad says, standing in front of the three of us. He rests his hands on Luca and my shoulders, his eyes moving between us. "This is going to be the hardest two months of your lives. But I have prepared you. After a day on the island, you'll want to leave. Stay strong. The struggle is worth it in the end."

"Any advice for us?" Bash asks, shifting his stance to his right foot, clearly nervous about going to the island.

"You're a Salvatore," Dad says to each of us individually, "Make them fear the name I gave you."

My heart swells at his words. Our adoptive father is mean and sort of terrifying, but he's my dad and has been for the past ten years. I have been his son longer than I was Damian Townsend. My biological father is almost a distant memory at this point.

So when Arlo calls us his sons—calls us Salvatores—it means something to me. That's why I will do anything he asks. Disappointing him is not an option. I want to be part of this family, and so does Bash.

He gives each of us a one-arm hug.

"Good luck," he tells us. "I'll be watching from a distance."

Marcello is beside our dad and tips his head. There is no love lost with Luca and Marcello and definitely no hugging. Luca doesn't even look back as he climbs into the limo.

Bastian gets in next.

I step toward the door, but Dad grabs my arm.

"Damian, you're special," he says, his voice low but deep. "You will have the easiest time on the island. The things I have taught you… Use those skills to survive. Understand?"

My hunting skills.

I nod. "Yes, sir."

"Good boy." He pats my back. "Take care of your brothers. Bash will need you the most."

He doesn't realize that I need Bash even more than he needs me. But that part of our relationship we never talk about. Luca and Marcello know, so I'm sure our dad does, too. However, he's never confronted us about it.

"I'll take care of them," I promise before I slip into the limo with my brothers.

THE SCENERY BELOW US IS BREATHTAKING. NOTHING BUT BLUE-green water for miles. I know the island is somewhere off the Atlantic Ocean. But I'm not sure where the hell they are taking us.

When we're about to land on the island, I lean over and

wrap my arm around Bash. "We'll get through this together," I whisper in his ear. "It's you and me. Forever."

The rotary blades are so loud it's hard to hear over them.

He presses his lips to my ear and says, "Always." His hand grazes my thigh, and I wish he would keep it there but pulls away immediately, knowing Luca is watching us. "Two months. We can make it, D."

I know we will.

Or die trying.

There's no way in hell I will disappoint my father. I don't care if they starve us to death because the three of us will find a way to survive.

As our bodies separate, Luca is glaring at us. He doesn't have an issue with us being into each other. But he does have a problem with us showing what he considers unnecessary affection. I don't think he's ever hugged Marcello. In fact, he tried to kill him a bunch of times when they were kids.

"If you two act like pussies on this island," Luca hisses, shaking his head. "I'm disowning you."

The helicopter lands and the door opens. Luca takes one look at us and hops down from the chopper without another word.

"Fucking asshole," Bash mumbles, hand balled into a fist on his lap. "I might kill him before we leave this goddamn island."

Chapter Seventeen

THERE'S BLOOD. SO MUCH FUCKING BLOOD AND THE AIR smells like metal. It's all I can think about, consumed by the bloodlust. My heart races uncontrollably, clambering in my chest.

I need Bash.

But he can't fix me, not in the way I need him to. Not with all of The Devil's Knights in our pledge class surrounding us.

He's forced to watch me lose my mind, kneeling on the ground and tearing through organs. Right through the muscle. Discarding the bones like a vulture picking apart the scraps of a corpse.

They made me do this.

I didn't have a choice.

I have to survive.

For him.

For *them*.

TWO MONTHS LATER, WE COME HOME FROM SKULL ISLAND bruised and battered. We're not the same men. Our father was right about that.

As the three of us exit the limousine, our father waits for

us on the front steps. Dressed in a black Brioni suit, he grins, which is unusual. He rarely smiles, but today he can't contain his excitement. A man of few words, Arlo pulls each of us into a one-arm hug, starting with Luca and saving me for last.

I'm everyone's last choice.

Always.

"My boys," Dad says, leading us into the house. "You did well on the island. I watched all the footage and couldn't be more proud of you."

I cast a sideways glance at Bash. He shakes his head, disgusted with himself for all of the horrible shit our pledge class was forced to do in the name of The Devil's Knights.

I'd killed plenty of men, but this time, it was different. The prisoners on the island were vile criminals. But the "bonding" exercises were the worst. We could only complete tasks as a group. Most of the time, that meant enduring hellish conditions without food or water. Sleeping in filth and blood with rats clawing at our skin in the darkness.

Dad ushers us into the sitting room, stopping in front of the bar to pour himself a glass. He hands one to each of us, and we salute to us becoming Knights. We have four more months of the six-month training. But we can finish the next part while we're at Harvard.

I'm not the same man who left Devil's Creek two months ago. The shit they put us through on the island changed all of us. Even Bash isn't very talkative, and he's usually the most normal of the three of us. He's been reserved and hasn't spoken much, not even on the plane ride home.

Luca took everything they threw at him in stride and never complained. It didn't matter what our pledge class was forced to do, he did it. We all did, but even I was ready to throw in the towel a few times. If not for Bash, I don't know if I would have made it. I'm not sure he would have lasted that long without me either.

Our dad's phone rings, and he leaves the room to answer

the call. Business as usual, he never takes a day off. It doesn't matter that it's Sunday. Doesn't matter he hasn't seen us in months. Arlo Salvatore loves money more than anything in this world.

Luca kicks his feet up on the table, leaning back in the armchair like a king. "We're not visiting Alex in Providence." He drinks from the high ball glass, downing half the contents. "No calls. No texts. No contact. And by the time she sees us again, she'll be compliant."

She left our estate after Bash kissed her, refusing to speak to Luca. Her act of rebellion set Luca off before we left, and he's been stewing over it ever since.

Luca hates her again.

"Alex texted me earlier," Bash tells him.

"Me, too," I add.

Luca nods. "Yeah, I got her text. But I don't care what she has to say."

He's going to make her life a living hell, and this time, he will use us to help him. We're always pulled into his plans.

"Get over yourself," Bash snaps. "You fucked with her head and screwed us over in the process. Alex has every right to be mad at you."

"I don't give a fuck." Luca drains the glass and slams it on the table, eyeing up Bash with those cold, blue eyes. "She needs to learn her place. That girl has gotten away with too much shit because the two of you let her. You went fucking soft on me in high school. That's why I laid my claim to her. I did that for both of you."

Bash shoots up from the couch, cheeks flushed with anger. "I'm not in the mood for your shit right now, Luca." He turns his back to us, walking toward the exit. "I need a fucking shower and a nap before I can talk to you."

I'm left alone with Luca's miserable ass since Dad hasn't returned.

Luca gives me one of his challenging glares that says, *Are you going to run like a scared bitch, too?*

So I stay.

I'm not afraid of him.

"You'll do what's necessary." Luca rests his elbow on the armchair, eying me up. "Talk some sense into Bash. This is the smart move. Alex needs to learn her place. No more babying her. No more treating her like a spoiled princess. If she's to become the Queen of The Devil's Knights, we need her to toughen up."

He has a point.

Our girl isn't ready to become our queen. But one day, she will be, and she has to learn how to swim on her own.

Chapter Eighteen

Eighteen months later...

IT'S BEEN TOO LONG SINCE WE WERE IN THE SAME ROOM AS Alex. Well, too long since she's known we were there.

But tonight is a special occasion.

Alex has finally stopped waiting for us to make an appearance in Providence. She hasn't texted us, asking when she will see us again.

We ignored her texts.

Sent the calls to voicemail.

What we're doing to her is borderline psychotic. It's all part of the mind games Luca likes to play with her. He enjoys watching her squirm, and sometimes, I do, too.

I'm sitting at a table with Luca and Bash, hanging out in the corner of the room away from the other students. Alex hasn't noticed us yet. My pretty little Pet is at the bar, drinking a craft beer with an artsy-looking guy. He's wearing ripped jeans, sneakers, and a white T-shirt that has colored graffiti on it.

The polar opposite of me.

He reminds me of Aiden Wellington. But this guy has short, brown hair that flops onto his forehead. He's kind of nerdy and gives off weird vibes.

Well, so do I.

Alex has been hanging out with this guy a lot lately. From

what we've read of her texts, listened to her calls, and monitored her computer, she hasn't kissed him yet. But she's been thinking about it. She's upset that we left her and feels abandoned.

In our defense, we were at college, trying to pass our classes while dealing with Knights business. Our lives are not simple and never will be. We can't have normal college student lives because we're not normal.

After our initiation into The Devil's Knights, Luca made a pact with all of us. Even Marcello, who he doesn't even like. He said the four of us could share Alex in every way as long as we followed his rules.

Luca needs the marriage.

Marcello wants a baby.

Bastian wants her cherry.

And I want *them*.

We took a blood oath and promised not to fuck over the other. If Bash wants her virginity, then all of us have to be there. But none of us can get in the way of Alex marrying Luca. Marcello will get the kid he's so desperate to have with her.

Not sure why but Marcello really wants to be a father. He's kinda young to be a dad. But whatever. I don't care as long as I get Bash and Alex in the end.

I'll share her.

Teach her.

Luca gets up from the table, his eyes on Alex. "It's time. She needs to know who owns her. And it's definitely not that loser."

We approach Alex as a team, and with her back to us, she has no idea we're coming. The artsy guy drinks from his beer and then puts his hand on Alex's thigh. I think about snapping his wrist in multiple places, so he can't use his hand again.

Luca grips the guy by the shoulder and yanks him off the bar stool.

"Hey, what the fuck?" Alex's date throws up his hands in front of his face like he's ready to fight. But judging by his frame, he wouldn't land one punch on any of us. "Who the fuck do you think you are, asshole?"

Luca gets in his face, his eyes menacing and intense. "I'm her fiancé." He grips the man by his shirt collar. "And if you ever touch my woman again, I'll kill you and feed your entrails to my fish."

"Luca!" Alex flies off the stool and shoves her palms into his back. "Get off him! I'm not your fucking fiancée, you psycho."

"You *are* mine, Drea." His top lip curls up into a snarl. "I let you have your fun at college. But I have been watching you, baby girl."

"Look, man," the guy says, hands raised. "I didn't know she was yours."

"I'm not," Alex interjects, moving between Luca and her date. "Tom, I'm sorry. He's a lunatic who thinks he can control my life. We're not together."

"Yes, we are." Luca slides his arm across her stomach and pulls her back into his chest. He dips his head down and brushes her earlobe with his lips. "You're going to be my wife."

"No, I'm not," she hisses. "That ship has sailed."

"Sorry, Alex," Tom says. "But I'm gonna go. I don't want to be in the middle of this."

"Wait," she says as he turns his back to her. "Don't leave. Ignore him. We still have to talk about our group project."

Tom moves through the crowd and exits the bar without looking back.

"I hate you!" Alex shouts. "Fuck you and your stupid fucking games, Luca. I waited over a year for the three of you to visit me. No return phone calls or texts. I'm done with all of you and your bullshit."

She attempts to leave.

I throw my arm out in front of her. "You're not leaving us, Pet."

Alex flicks her long, blonde curls over her shoulder and scoffs. "Fuck you, Damian. I'm not *yours*. Not anymore."

"You're *mine*." I bend down to her height, sliding my hand beneath her chin. "*Ours*. Stop denying it, Pet."

She sighs, her shoulders sinking. "Why haven't you answered any of my texts?"

"Been busy," I lie.

"Same," Bash agrees. "But we've been watching you, Cherry. We always know what you're doing."

She laughs, but it's forced. "Well, that's not at all romantic or comforting."

Luca steps closer, so the three of us have her boxed in with nowhere to go. "If I have to come back here and dispose of that loser's body, you're not going to like the punishment, Drea."

"What?" Alex chokes on her words. "Are you serious? Tom is my partner for a group project. We can't complete it without the other, or we both fail."

"You like him," Luca tells her because he already knows from reading her text messages and listening to her conversations with Aiden. "And if you think about kissing him or doing *anything* with him, I *will* kill him."

"Wow," she mouths, shaking her head. "Fucking crazy asshole."

"Yeah, baby girl. I am crazy." He yanks on her curls, his lips inches from hers. "Crazy about you and protecting what is mine."

"I'm not yours, Luca. You don't even want me." She sighs, lowering her eyes. "That much you made perfectly clear at your graduation party. And it's been over a fucking year since that night, asshole."

He slides the pad of his thumb across her bottom lip, smearing the red lipstick. "If anyone who doesn't have the last name Salvatore kisses these lips, I will cut them off and shove them down their throat. Do you understand me, Drea?"

She rolls her eyes. "So I can kiss your brothers?"

He nods.

"Any of them?"

Another nod.

She folds her arms over her chest. "Even Marcello?"

"Yes," he bites out. "Were you not listening to me, woman?"

"You know," Alex says, twirling a curl around her finger. "Your dad is kinda hot for an older man. Maybe I'll kiss him, too." A smirk pulls at her pretty mouth. "Since you guys have the same last name and all."

She's just trying to piss Luca off. I love how she pushes his buttons and finds ways to get under his skin. No one really challenges him. Marcello does sometimes, but we usually just go with the flow and let Luca take charge.

It's easier that way.

"You could try," Luca fires back, his eyebrows pinched together in frustration. "But I doubt you'd get very far with our father."

She inches her hands up Luca's chest and wraps her arms around his neck. "How about you, Luca? You say I'm yours, but you haven't kissed me."

"I don't like kissing," he admits.

"Why not?" Alex wets her lips, keeping her eyes on his. "Don't you want to claim what's *yours*?"

"Don't play games with me, Drea." He cups her cheek, but it's not a sweet gesture. His thumb digs into her cheek, pushing into the bone. "I don't like when you act like a brat."

"Well, I don't like when you fuck with my head. So I guess we're even." She stands on her tippy toes, tightening her grip around his neck. "Kiss me, Luca. If you don't, I'll never let you touch me again."

Luca hates ultimatums.

He's always the one in control, but with Alex, he often concedes without admitting defeat. He stopped fucking cheerleaders after she challenged him. And if the past is any indication of the present, he's going to kiss her now.

And he does.

Luca clutches her face, licking along the seam of her mouth until she opens up for him. Her tits mold to his chest, and I love how much weight she's gained since high school. Now, she has the body of a woman and nice, big tits that I can't wait to fuck.

As expected, Luca is aggressive and kisses her like he's in physical pain. Maybe he is. Because I can see the hesitation on his face with each kiss. But he's not pulling away, not showing her how this much intimacy is killing him.

I wonder if I will look the same when I finally kiss her. Will it seem like I hate it? I can't imagine kissing her would repulse me. Not after seeing how she made Bash feel.

I want to know how she tastes. She always smells good enough to eat.

Sweet like candy.

Luca pulls away first, and they're both breathless, gazing into each other's eyes as if seeing each other for the first time. Does he feel it now? The strong pull each of us has felt toward her since day one. It's taken Luca much longer than the rest of us.

He still hates her for what happened in the past. But Alex is not her mother, and she didn't kill Evangeline Franco. Even Marcello has let go of his anger toward her.

"Was that so bad?" Alex asks Luca, clinging to his chest like a koala.

I can tell she doesn't want to let go of him.

Luca doesn't answer her. Instead, he takes her hand and drags her away from the bar. "It's time for bed."

She's slightly drunk and wobbling. Her hand crashes into my chest to brace her weight before she falls on her ass.

"You drank too much, Cherry." Bastian strokes her cheek with his fingers. "You need to eat."

"Are you staying in Providence for the night?" Alex asks no one in particular as we leave the bar together.

Luca shakes his head. "We're going back to Cambridge."

"No," she says, slurring her words. "Stay the night."

Alex is always desperate for more of us. But we need to leave, and she's not going to like it when we do. Because this is the last time she will see us for a while.

Without us nearby, it will keep the target off her back. She's in more danger around us, so we've left her alone. Let her have a normal college life.

Years from now, she may hate us. She may even blame us for a lot of things that are out of our control. But in the end, she will be ours.

I know it.

My brothers know it.

So until then…

We wait.

Chapter Nineteen

One year later...

I'M NEVER FAR FROM ALEX. HUNTING IS MY SPECIALTY, AND when I set my sights on my prey, I have laser focus.

I lean against the brick wall, the darkness obscuring my body. Waiting in the shadows, I stare across the street at her apartment building. Students pass by on their way across campus. It's after ten o'clock, and the parties are in full swing.

Alex hasn't dated anyone while attending RISD. Not even a single kiss. She shares an apartment with her twin and mostly keeps to herself. But tonight, she's having company.

Two girls from her art class and one of Aiden's friends. I hate that a man is in her apartment right now getting to look at her. I hate knowing he's staring at her, thinking about doing disgusting things to her.

Whenever she's gotten too close to a man, one of us put a stop to it. Death threats are incredibly motivating reasons not to touch our girl. If necessary, I will kill Aiden's friend. Anyone who gets in my way will be eliminated.

Last night, we received intel that men were looking for the heirs to the Wellington fortune. And since I don't mind killing her enemies, I volunteered to drive to Providence.

Luca is in Cambridge, holding court for the new members of The Devil's Knights. He's popular everywhere he goes.

Despite being a world-class dickhead, Luca never has a problem getting people to follow him.

The girls on campus flock to him, begging for one minute of his time. It's like high school all over again. And I'm the brother everyone fears.

No one speaks to me.

No one looks at me.

They know better.

I like it that way.

Around midnight, Alex leaves the apartment with two brunette girls and a boy with black hair. He's thin and tall, with a pointy nose, and wearing faded jeans and a band T-shirt.

This guy isn't her type.

Alex doesn't pay him any attention and waves without looking at him. He heads in the opposite direction.

The girls cross the street and turn left toward a bar. I push off the wall, keeping my distance, listening to their conversation as I trail behind them.

"You should have a drink with us," the girl on Alex's right says. "I want you to meet Kieran."

"Yeah," the other girl says. "Just one drink. It won't kill you."

"I can't." Alex gives her a sweet but forced smile. "Aiden is waiting for me at home. Maybe next time."

The girl bobs her head. "If you change your mind, we'll be here until two."

Alex waits until they enter the bar and sighs. She brushes the blonde curls off her forehead, shoving them out of her pretty, blue eyes. I see the longing on her face and know how she feels. It's hard not being like everyone else.

Carl Wellington warned his grandchildren to be careful on campus. He didn't give them the specifics about the danger, but he did alert them.

I don't bother hiding when she spins around, flicking the

curls over her shoulder. Startled, she gasps, her hand flying up to cover her mouth.

"Hello, Pet." I slide my fingers beneath her chin and pull her closer. "Did you miss me?"

She drops her hand to her side and blinks as if she doesn't believe I'm really here. "Damian?"

Curling my arm around her, I feel the delicious curves of her perfect body. She's no longer the skinny girl we met in high school. Alex has big tits, thick thighs, and a sweet ass I dig my fingers into.

Her lips part as I grip her tighter. "What are you doing in Providence?"

I lift her into my arms and lead her into the dark alley, pressing her back against the wall. "I'm keeping the monsters away."

She blows out a breath of air and seems disappointed by my response. "Then who will save me from you?"

"Aww, Pet." I stroke her cheek. "Don't act like you don't enjoy playing with monsters."

"I'm still mad at you." She shoves her palms into my chest. "You left me again. All of you did. And you didn't even have the decency to return any of my calls or texts."

I grab a fistful of her hair and yank her toward me. "I'm here now, Pet." I lick my lips when our eyes meet. "Now be a good girl and stop acting like an ungrateful brat."

She scoffs, swats at my hand, and attempts to get out of my grasp. But I love when she squirms and strengthen my hold on her.

"Damian, please." Alex peeks up at me, tucking her lip into her mouth, and gives me a pouty face. "Don't be an asshole."

"You didn't answer my question, Pet." I run the pad of my thumb across her lip and breathe in the sweet scent of her perfume. "Did you miss me?"

I know she did.

I want her to say it.

I *need* to hear it.

Her cell phone rings, and she holds my gaze, reaching into her jeans pocket to look at the Caller ID.

It's her twin brother.

"Lexie, where are you?" I can hear Aiden say on the other end.

I still hate his nickname for her. It doesn't match Alex at all.

"I'm coming home now, Aid." She holds the phone against her shoulder, rolling her eyes at me. "Be there in a minute."

She stuffs the phone into her pocket. "I have to go, Damian. Put me down."

"No." I lean into her, our mouths so close that our lips nearly brush. "I drove all the way over here to see you." I sniff her hair and drink in her delicious scent. She always smells like candy. "I need to touch you. Taste you."

"Oh, God," she whispers. "Damian."

I love when she says my name in that deep but sultry voice. Only Bash makes my cock as hard as she does.

"When was the last time a man made you come?"

I know the answer but want her to confirm it.

She digs her teeth into her bottom lip, staring at my mouth. "I don't know. I guess when you and Bash touched me in high school."

"You haven't been with anyone else?"

My girl shakes her head. "Just you and Bash. And that one time Luca kissed me."

"Good girl," I praise, stroking my fingers through her blonde curls. "It will stay that way until we can be together again, understood?"

"Why all the games, Damian?" Alex sighs. "I don't get it. Why did you leave me? Why haven't any of you answered my calls, texts, or emails? I wanted to see you for close to three years. And I got nothing."

I rest my forehead against hers, loving the feel of her skin against mine. It's been too long since I touched her. Too fucking long since I got to hold my girl and play with her.

"Do you want the truth?"

I can give this to her.

Luca will be mad that I talked to her.

Don't care.

He can fuck off.

I don't answer to him.

Luca will be the Grand Master of The Devil's Knights one day, but I'm not here on Knights business.

This is personal.

Alex nods. "Please, tell me why. I need to know, so I can stop feeling like I did something wrong."

"Baby, you did nothing wrong."

I stare at her pretty face, surprised by the name I called her. It sounded good as it rolled off my tongue, but I prefer Pet.

Pet suits her.

She has a thin neck that will look good with my collar on it someday. It will happen, eventually. I already picked out a diamond choker for her.

"You're in danger with us," I confess, feeling the weight lift off my chest at keeping this secret from her for too long. "The Salvatores have a lot of enemies. So do The Devil's Knights. And if you were seen with us, it would only make your life worse."

"My family has enemies, too." A frown tugs at her mouth. "But you don't see my grandfather not talking to Aiden and me over it."

"It's not that simple," I explain. "Without us, you get to live your life in Providence. You get to be normal. Those girls you hang out with wouldn't be safe around you otherwise. We are doing this *for* you. Not *to* you. Do you understand me?"

Alex hooks her arms around my neck and presses her plump lips to my jaw, leaving a trail of hot kisses on my skin. "I missed you. But I'm still mad at you. At all of you." She stops kissing me and looks into my eyes as if she's searching for something. "Please pass the message along to your asshole brothers."

Her phone rings again.

"Damian, I really have to go. My brother worries about me."

She attempts to fish the phone from her pocket, but I beat her to it and answer.

"Aiden, your sister is with me. Stop fucking calling."

"Damian?" Aiden sounds confused.

"Alex is safe. She'll be home when I'm done talking to her. Don't call again."

I hang up and hand her the phone.

"You are such a dick," she groans, stuffing the phone back into her pocket.

I set her feet on the ground and unbutton her jeans, shoving them down her legs. "A dick who's going to make you come."

Chapter Twenty

ALEX'S EYES WIDEN AT MY WORDS, EXCITEMENT FLASHING across her face. She strips off the right leg of her pants to give me better access.

I take the hunting knife from the inner pocket of my suit jacket and hold it out in front of her. "Remember this?"

She nods, a smile slowly spreading across her face. "Do you have new panties for me?"

"I'll send you something after I leave."

"I don't want you to leave." Alex grips my tie between her fingers and pulls me closer. "Stay with me tonight."

She practically begged us to fuck her in high school. But because of Luca's stupid fucking rules, our girl is still a virgin. If I stay tonight, she will give me her virginity.

I know it.

But Bash wants to pop her cherry too badly for me to take that away from him.

"I can't stay. I have to get back to Cambridge."

Clutching her thigh, I wrap her leg around my back and cut her panties off her body, tucking them into my pocket for later. Then I slide two fingers into her pussy.

"I drove here to make sure you're okay. And now, I can leave, knowing you're not only safe but satisfied."

"Since when do you care about my needs?" Alex teases.

"Have I ever left you hanging?" I bend down to meet her

height and raise an eyebrow. "Huh? Name one time I didn't let you come."

She can't.

It's been almost three years since I felt her tight cunt squeeze my fingers like this, and I'm ready to lose my mind. My cock is so hard it's straining against my pants, poking her stomach.

"Fuck, you feel good," I groan, pulling my fingers out and adding another one. "Just as tight as I remember. Now, be a good girl and squeeze my fingers."

She does as I instruct, and I wish it were my cock she strangled with her sweet pussy.

Alex moans, her sole focus on me as I pump my fingers faster, rolling my thumb over her clit. "I want to touch you."

"Go ahead." I tip my head at my raging hard-on. "You're a big girl. Show me you know what to do with my cock."

She's nervous and fumbles with the button on my slacks. I like watching her mentally freak out as she unzips my pants and fists my shaft through the slit in my boxer briefs.

"I like your dick," she says in a soft tone, curling her small hand around me to get a better grip. "It's really nice."

I laugh, which is rare for me. "Dicks are not nice, Pet. And neither is what I wanna do to you."

"Do it," she challenges, stroking my dick harder. "Fuck me, Damian. I know you want to." She gasps when I slam another finger into her tight channel, filling her up good. "I'm twenty-one and still a virgin." Taking the head of my cock, she rubs it against her slickness. "Move your hand. I want to put you inside me."

I shake my head. "Not tonight, Pet. I'm not taking your virginity in a dirty alley. You're too good for that."

I can't tell her that Bash would kill me. He would never speak to me again if I fucked her.

So I can't.

I won't.

Her shoulders slump against the wall, deflated by my response. She looks so miserable, even with my fingers filling her up to my knuckles. So I pull my fingers out of her, not wanting to leave her like this. One day, she's going to be mine and Bash's girl. And I want her to be happy.

I knock her hand away from my dick. "I have a better idea."

She gives me a sexy smile. "Change your mind?"

"Nope." I lift her up. "Wrap your legs around me."

Her arms go around my neck at the same time as her legs come around me, her heels digging into my ass.

"I'm not taking your virginity. But I'll give you something to think about when you're alone at night in bed and fingering your pussy."

She gasps when I drag the tip of my dick up and down her wet slit. "Oh, God, Damian."

"Feel good, Pet?"

"So good," she moans, shivering in my arms.

I can't fuck up and go any farther with her. If her hymen isn't intact when we take her virginity as a group, Bash will hate me. And our future plans for her are too good to waste on a quick fuck.

"Play with your clit," I order because I need to focus on not taking more than an inch. "Let me watch you unravel for me."

Like a good pet, she listens, rubbing her clit with her thumb.

It's so fucking hard.

So.

Fucking.

Hard.

Her pussy is soft and wet, and it would be so easy to slide the rest of the way in and claim her. Alex rocks her hips, greedy for more, which pushes another inch of me into her.

"Calm down, Pet." I yank her hair and force her to look at

me. "Let me do the work. Keep playing with your clit. I want to feel you explode on my cock."

She settles into a good rhythm with me, moaning in my ear as she drips cum onto my cock. I lap up her juices and use them to lubricate my skin, making it even harder for me to hold off any longer.

"I'm coming," she whimpers. "Damian. Oh. God."

"Come for me, Pet," I choke out and pull back right before a steam of cum shoots out of my dick, coating her pretty pussy lips.

Breathless, she glances down at the mess we've made, and then her gaze goes back to my face. Alex nibbles on her bottom lip. "Are you sure you can't stay the night?"

As if on cue, my cell phone rings with the ringtone that is specific to Bastian. It's like he knows I was so close to fucking our girl and is jealous he's not here to get in on the action.

I set her on the ground and hold the phone up to my ear. "Yeah?"

"Don't yeah me," Bastian hisses into the phone, his words slightly slurred. "I haven't heard from you in two hours."

He sounds a little drunk.

"I'm with Alex," I tell him. "She's okay."

"Who is that?"

She's already fixed her panties back into place and pulls her jeans up her thighs.

"Is that my sweet Cherry?"

"It's Bash."

She holds out her hand. "Let me talk to him."

I hand her the phone. "Hey." A smile turns up the corners of her mouth as he talks. "Yeah, I miss you. Duh. Why didn't you come with Damian?"

As I tuck my cock back into my pants and zip up, I watch the joy spread across her face. She cares about Bash as much as he does her.

"I want to see you." A pause. "Um, okay." Her eyes flick up at me. "He's calling us on FaceTime."

A second later, the phone rings. She raises the screen in front of her face and smiles as Bash appears. I move beside her so he can see both of us.

"Hey, D. Taking good care of our girl, I hope."

"Of course." I wink. "She just came all over my cock."

"What?" His eyes widen in shock. "Please tell me you didn't."

"We didn't have sex," Alex explains. "But I got to feel Damian inside me."

"We will talk about this later," he snaps at me, his eyes hooded from drinking too much.

He looks so fucking hot, with his caramel brown hair all messed up like he's been tugging at the ends. His shirt is off, and from the looks of it, he's spread out on his bed.

We share an off-campus house at Harvard University, where we let other Knights live with us. I hate sharing space with strangers. But it's all part of The Devil's Knights' bonding experience.

"I want to see you in person, Bash."

"Baby, I'm drunk and can barely walk down the stairs." He leans back on a stack of pillows, holding the phone out. "Another time, yeah?"

"Yeah," she agrees. "But it better not be two more years from now. I'm sick of waiting around on you."

"It won't be," he promises. "I miss you, Cherry. Every single day I'm here, and you're there. I think about your wet, tight pussy every time I jerk off. Think about your sexy lips and those big tits. Fuck, baby. You look so hot."

She giggles, a blush dusting her cheeks. "I'm not even dressed up and don't have on any makeup."

"You don't need it," he says, and I agree with his analysis. "My dick is hard just looking at you."

"Bash," Luca yells from a distance before barging into his room, slamming the door so hard it hits the wall. "Get downstairs. This isn't fucking playtime."

"Luca," Alex says in a hopeful tone.

Bash turns the phone around so she can see Luca, who looks like he's ready to explode with rage. He inches toward the bed, his dark blue eyes wide with fury.

"You broke my fucking rules, asshole." He snatches the phone from Bash's hand.

"Fuck you," Bash shoots back, reaching for the phone.

"Damian, get home now," Luca hisses. "The three of us need to talk. You clearly don't know how to fucking listen."

He doesn't acknowledge Alex before he hangs up.

Alex huffs. "What was that about?"

There's no point in explaining Luca's complexities, so I take the phone from her and shrug. "I don't know, Pet. But I gotta go."

She doesn't protest when I grab her hand and lead her across the street. I walk her up to the second floor and stop in front of the apartment she shares with Aiden.

Alex hesitates, looking at me as she touches the handle. "When will I see you again?"

"I don't know," I say truthfully.

"Luca is mad at you and Bash, isn't he?"

I nod to confirm.

"Is he the reason you don't talk to me?"

Another nod.

"I hate him," she chokes out.

Sometimes, I do, too.

But I can't tell her that.

I'm a Salvatore and have to maintain a united front with my brothers. Our father instilled that in us from a young age.

Alex stands on her tippy toes and kisses my cheek. "Bye, Damian."

I kiss her head, getting a good whiff of her shampoo, and attempt to memorize her scent as I dig my fingers into her thick ass. "Bye, Pet."

Chapter Twenty-One

One year later...

'M GETTING SICK OF WAITING. TIRED OF NOT HAVING MY GIRL and Bash. The need to consume them is stronger than my desire to kill. It has been seeping into my skin, clawing at my insides and making my black heart even blacker.

I need *them*.

After the night I almost fucked Alex, Bash and I got into a fistfight with Luca over it. We all walked away with cuts and bruises. And the next day, we agreed we couldn't allow a woman to separate us.

So I didn't see Alex again.

I kept my distance when I went to Providence to check on her. A few times, I caught men sniffing around by her apartment and introduced them to my hunting knife.

Bash is with me this time.

We got a tip that some Russian scumbag was searching for the heirs to the Wellington fortune. So far, I haven't seen anyone who doesn't live in her building coming and going all day. We have a list of every student and have done our homework.

"Time for a break." Bash pushes off from the brick wall. 'I'm starving. Call Marcello and ask him to take over while we

Marcello assists with Alex's surveillance since he opted out of college. He stayed in Devil's Creek to help our father run Alpha Command, a team of mercenaries who work for Salvatore Global off the books.

I reach into my pocket and text Marcello. He responds immediately and says he has eyes on Alex. If only she knew how much of her we can see daily. She'd probably be mortified to know we have cameras everywhere. We read all of her texts, listen to all of her phone calls, and intercept every email.

But it's for her protection.

She's been sheltered for most of her life and is too trusting of people. Look at how easily she trusted us, and we're fucking snakes. But at least we give a damn about her.

I have killed for her.

I would do *anything* for her.

Bash pats me on the back, shoving me down the street toward his car. "Before we leave, I want to see her. Even if it's only for a minute. I don't care what we promised Luca."

I nod. "Luca's not here. What he doesn't know won't kill him."

We get into his Porsche and drive to an Italian restaurant in downtown Providence. They're booked solid for the night, but all it takes is mentioning our father's name, and we get a table at the back of the restaurant.

Being a Salvatore opens doors. Our father goes way back with the owner, who is connected to the Sicilian Mafia.

I get into the booth beside Bash and scan the menu, already knowing what I want to order. The waitress arrives, and we send her away to grab a bottle of their best red wine while Bash takes his sweet-ass time deciding on what to eat.

"Just pick something."

I tap the platinum and onyx ring on the table beside his hand. The black chips form a serpent that represents the Salvatore crest. Our father gave them to us when we became Knights. I'd never seen him look so proud.

"You pick." Bastian hands me the menu. "I'm sick of making decisions."

He's annoyed with his grandfather, who called before we left to spy on Alex. We were having a good day until the old man had to give his two cents about Bash and his life.

Nothing is ever good enough. It doesn't matter that Bash has straight As and will make a good CEO of Atlantic Airlines after we graduate. Bastian could turn water into wine, and Fitzy would say, *Is that all you can do?*

I put my hand on top of his. "Don't worry about that old bastard. He's only trying to fuck with your head."

Bastian's nostrils flare. "I fucking hate him. I wish he would die already and stay the fuck out of my business."

"He'll probably live forever just to torture you," I joke, but he doesn't find it funny.

The waitress arrives with our wine and pours us a glass. She flashes a smile at us, staring like she's wondering how we would look naked. I know I'm good-looking. It's not like I don't own a mirror. But I only want one woman—and this girl is not Alex.

Not even close.

So I slip my fingers between Bash's on the table to give her the hint to fuck off. Her eyes lower to our joined hands. As if she now gets the message, she sets the wine on the table and takes a step back.

"What can I get you, gentleman?"

I hand her the menus. "We'll both have the eggplant caponata."

"I'm not in the mood for stew," Bash complains as she walks away.

"You're not in the mood for anything," I fire back. "So sit there and be quiet if you're going to act like a baby."

He sticks out his tongue at me, and it reminds me of when we were kids. Whenever Bash didn't get his way, he would act out. I have tried all day to cheer him up.

Nothing is working.

Bash leans into my arm and slides his hand onto my thigh. "You know what would make me feel better?"

I turn my head to look at him. "My lips wrapped around your cock?"

"Hmmm…" He licks his lips. "Yes to that later. But I was thinking Alex's pussy will make this day all better."

"She's only ten minutes away," I remind him. "And I know she's dying to see you. Her brother won't be home for a few hours. We'll have her all to ourselves."

His eyes trace my lips as he licks his. "After we eat, we're claiming our girl. The hell with Luca."

I LEAN AGAINST THE DOORFRAME AS ALEX OPENS IT, SURPRISE scrolling across her beautiful face.

"Hello, Pet."

"Damian?" Her gaze flicks from me to Bastian. "Bash?"

Those big blue eyes water and I can't tell if she's happy or sad. But then she launches herself into Bash's arms, clinging to his muscular body.

"Bash." She kisses his cheek, then his jaw before looking into his eyes. "Oh. My. God." Another kiss to his nose. "You're really here."

It's been two years since she last saw him. And back then, they barely touched. That was the night she kissed Luca at the bar before we put her drunk ass to bed.

Bastian has been jerking off to surveillance pictures of her for years. I know he needs her in his life and hates being separated from her. Sometimes when we fuck around, we role-play and pretend Alex is with us. That Alex is sucking our cocks.

He palms the back of her head and holds her in his arms. "I'm here." His lips press against her forehead as he carries her into the living room. "I missed you, Cherry."

I take one last look into the hallway and slide the deadbolt into place. There are three locks on her door because we can't be too careful with her safety. If anything were to happen to her, it would kill Bash and me. I don't know if Bash would ever recover. So I never let Alex out of my sight. Our girl is my number one priority.

"I missed you, too." She latches onto his neck and sits back to look at him. "The last time Damian was here, he said Luca wouldn't let you see me."

Bastian swallows hard, his Adam's apple bobbing. "It's complicated, baby."

"I hate him." Her head snaps to me, and she moves her hand from Bash's chest to my face. "I missed you, Damian."

I love hearing her say that.

"Did you miss me?" Alex asks when I don't respond.

I smear the gloss on her pretty, pink lips. "I missed these lips." I lean in and sniff her hair. "Missed your scent."

She gives me a playful smile. "That's all?"

I move behind her and grab her ass with both hands, covering Bash's big ones that are gripping her tight. "Missed this fat ass."

Alex giggles. "My ass isn't fat."

"Yes. It. Is." I squeeze her ass again. "I can't wait to fuck this ass."

A grin spreads across Bash's lips as our eyes meet, and I dip my head down to suck on her neck, keeping my gaze on him. "And this perfect neck I want to put a collar on. I missed this, too."

"Damian," she moans, her head rolling to the side and onto Bash's shoulder. "Mmm…"

"Are you still doubting how much I missed you, Pet?" My

hand moves between her and Bash, so I can cup her pussy over the black yoga pants. "Hmm? Tell me."

"I want you, Damian." She lifts her head from Bash's shoulder, lips parted. "You, too, Bash."

We haven't tagged-teamed her since high school. Excitement rushes through me. I have patiently waited to get both of them in the same room again. Because of Luca and his stupid fucking rules, we have been denying ourselves pleasure.

"Bedroom," I tell Bash.

He carries her down the hallway, with her chin on his shoulder and those big, blue eyes watching me. My God, I have missed her. And I never miss anyone. Alex and Bash are my exceptions.

They're *mine*.

Bastian lowers Alex to the mattress in her bedroom. He stands above her, waiting for me to join him as we strip off our suit jackets and throw them onto the bed.

"Fuck Luca," he whispers to me.

I nod. "Fuck 'em."

Alex's plump lips curl up into a smile. "I've dreamed about this for years." She leans back on her palms, legs spread wide for us. "It's going to hurt, isn't it?"

Bash puts one knee on the bed beside her, running his fingers up and down her inner thigh. "The first time will, yeah. But we'll take good care of your pussy."

I get on the other side of her, clutching her thigh with possession. My heart pounds, the blood humming in my veins as every inch of my skin sets on fire. "Pain feels good, Pet." I slide my hand closer to her core. "You'll see."

My monster wants to play.

And he wants blood.

Her blood.

A cell phone rings.

"What now?" Bash reaches into his pocket with a groan, holding the phone up to his ear. "This better be good, Marcello." A beat passes, and his jaw clenches. "Fuck, okay. Yeah, we're with her." He nods. "Uh-huh. Yep. Got it."

Bastian pockets the phone and lifts Alex from the bed, his eyes on me. "Incoming."

I know what he means.

She gives him a quizzical look. "What's going on?"

"Nothing, Cherry." He tips his head at the window, and I hear someone outside trying to get into her bedroom. "Make it clean."

I don't want clean.

I want to make a mess.

After he leaves the room with Alex, I shut the door and lock it. Then I shove the curtains to the side and open the window, startling the asshole who's trying to break into the apartment.

We were expecting him all night. Of course, he waits until we're about to fuck Alex to show up.

I grab the Russian piece of shit by the collar of his shirt and haul him through the window, throwing him onto the floor. He's dressed in a black suit that matches his hair that flops onto his tanned forehead. I don't recognize him. But I know he's Bratva.

Kneeling on the floor, I wrap my hands around his neck, wanting desperately to take out my hunting knife and slash his throat. The thought of blood splashing across my face thrills me.

But I can't make a mess.

Alex would be traumatized forever if she ever saw the kind of shit I did to the men who wanted to hurt her. The blood alone would haunt her dreams. So I choke the life out of this asshole.

"You ruined my night, you piece of shit." I curl my fingers tighter around his neck and squeeze, pinning him down with my legs when he tries to get out of my grasp. "We were so close." I shake my head, digging my knee into his chest. "And you had to go and fuck it all up."

The Russian Mafia wants to use Alex as leverage to get Bastian's cousin back. Grace Hale is Fitzy's only granddaughter and the heir to the Adams fortune. Her father is connected to the Bratva and the leader of the terrorist organization that killed our parents.

The Devil's Knights and The Founders Society have been keeping Grace safe since she was a child. Bastian has done a lot to protect the girl he's only met once. Before she became Grace Hale, she was Katarina Adams Romanov. Her name change was essential, but recently, The Lucaya Group discovered we have her. And ever since, we've had all kinds of criminals coming for us.

And now that they know about Alex, we have to get her out of here. No more easy college student life. She's going to have to pack tonight.

After the life drains from the man's eyes, I release my hold on his throat and rise from the floor. I find Alex in the living on top of Bash. He's cradling the back of her head and stroking his fingers through her hair.

"I will never let anyone hurt you," he promises before kissing her lips. "You're mine, Cherry. And I protect what's mine."

He does.

Bash has been protecting me from myself and the world for years.

"Where's your brother?" I ask Alex as I enter the room.

"At a friend's house." She turns to look at me. "Why?"

"Because he needs to come home and pack his shit. You're both moving out of this apartment tonight."

"W-What?" Alex croaks. "Are you serious?"

"Deadly," I tell her.

I reach into my pocket and grab my phone, sending a text to Marcello. He responds instantly, telling me that he will arrive in Providence with a security detail for Alex within the hour.

One of the perks of our father owning a private security firm is how quickly we are able to respond to threats. Marcello can take a short helicopter ride from Devil's Creek and be here with Alex when we have to leave.

We can't stay with her.

Chapter Twenty-Two

WITHIN TWO HOURS, WE HAVE ALEX AND AIDEN MOVED INTO A new apartment in Providence. It's more secure and not as close to the campus, but it will keep Alex safe for the next few months.

She's a wreck, shaking so hard from crying, terrified of someone coming for her again.

Marcello sits on the couch beside her and pulls her into his arms. "Look at me, princess." He hugs her against his chest. "You're safe. I'm here now."

Alex hasn't stopped crying since I killed the Russian. She doesn't understand what's going on, and we can't tell her everything. Some secrets have to stay with us.

Bastian held her on the couch until Marcello arrived, promising she was safe. No matter what we told her, she still wouldn't stop crying. I have never seen our girl this upset. She's always so tough and rough around the edges. It's like something snapped in her head.

"I'm staying in Providence," Marcello says to calm her down, running his long fingers up and down her back. "No one is going to hurt you."

"But that man," she bites out, her lip quivering. "He tried to climb through my window."

"He didn't touch you." He wipes away her tears with his thumb. "Damian took care of him."

"I know. But…" She sobs again, resting her head on his chest. "I'm scared."

"Look at me, Cherry." Bastian slips his fingers beneath her chin to steal her attention. "You're in a new apartment now. One with much better security. You have nothing to worry about, pretty girl. We got this covered. Aiden is here." He tips his head at her twin, who sits on the couch next to me. "And Marcello will be in the apartment next to yours until you graduate. If you need anything, he'll be there, okay?"

"You'll be safe, Lexie," Aiden promises. "I've got a gun and know how to use it."

"That's not as comforting as you may think, Aid." She sniffs away the tears. "I don't like guns. And I don't want one in our apartment."

"Too bad," Aiden tells her. "If another slimy Russian breaks in again, I'm shooting him in the skull. End of discussion."

I like that he's ride or die for his twin. We don't see eye-to-eye and have never gotten along, but Aiden isn't so bad. He will do anything in his power to protect Alex. That makes him alright in my book.

Ignoring her twin, Alex turns to look at Bash and wiggles her fingers. "I need you, Bash. Stay with me."

Alex has a special attachment to Bastian that she doesn't share with the rest of us. Even in high school, she clung to him. She thinks he's the *nicer* brother. But she doesn't know the real Bash, not like I do. He's different with her.

He takes Alex from Marcello and kisses her head. "I know you're scared, Cherry. But you need to put your big girl pants on. Stop with the tears."

She dabs at her cheeks. "I'm just freaked out. I haven't been this scared since I was a little girl."

Alex still has PTSD flashbacks and vivid nightmares of her awful childhood. It's the reason she has to share an apartment with Aiden. If he's not here to calm her down in the middle of the night, she will need to be hospitalized.

As long as Alex takes her medicine, she's usually okay. But tonight was too much for her. The threat set her over the edge, and she can't seem to calm down, no matter what any of us try.

"We have three months left of college," Bastian continues. "You'll be so busy working on the paintings for your art show you won't even notice we're gone."

"I'll be here for your art show," I tell her.

"So will I," Marcello adds.

Alex's eyes illuminate. "How about Luca?"

"I'll be there," Luca says, entering the living room as if he materialized out of thin air.

He said he was on his way thirty minutes ago, but he got here at record speed. Dressed impeccably in a black Brioni suit, Luca sits on the couch beside Bash and stares at Alex like he's ready to devour her.

"I invited a few of my mother's friends to look at your work," Luca says in his usual emotionless tone. "They can help launch your art career after graduation."

Alex hops off Bash's lap and leans into Luca's arm. "Really?"

"Yes." Luca rubs his thumb across her cheek to collect the tears. "But only if you stop crying and act like a queen."

She narrows her eyes at him. "I don't even know what that means, Luca."

"It means you need to toughen up. Do you think your life will be easy with me? With any of us?" Luca waits for her to shake her head before he says, "One day, you will be our queen. And we need you to be worthy of that title."

She has no idea what awaits her a few years from now. Her life is about to change forever.

"Luca," she coos, curling up against him, and surprisingly,

he doesn't push her away. "I have no idea what you're talking about."

He places his hand on her lower back and pulls her closer. "One day you will." With his free hand, he clutches her chin and swipes his thumb across her bottom lip. "One day, you will be mine, Drea. So I need you to learn how to stand on your own two feet. No more running to Bash for hugs. Or crying on Marcello's shoulder. Queens are powerful. Strong. They don't look to other people for help."

"Is this some kind of royalty role-play thing?" Alex laughs, tossing her curls over her shoulder. "Because I'm not following."

"I swear to God, woman," Luca hisses. "You drive me fucking crazy. No, we're not role-playing."

"Although, I do like the sound of that," Bash chimes, sliding his hand onto her hip. "I wanna play, baby."

"Seriously," Aiden groans. "Do you fucking mind? That's my sister." His jaw clenches. "Alex deserves better than this shit. She's not some toy for you and your brothers to pass around."

I like that Aiden has a pair of brass balls. But what I don't like is how he often speaks to my brothers and me with disrespect. Even after all these years of being a Wellington, he still hasn't lost the trashy attitude.

He doesn't look like the clean-cut heir to the Wellington fortune his grandfather wants him to be. Instead, Aiden has covered his body with black ink that he never hides. His artwork is plastered all over his body like he's a living mural. He rarely styles his short, blond curls so they're kind of a mess. And I have yet to see him in a pair of jeans that aren't ripped.

"Aid, it's not like that," Alex cuts in. "They're not passing me around."

He snorts. "Yeah. Fucking. Right. I know what I've seen and don't like it."

"Oh, please," she shoots back. "Don't get all high and mighty with me. I know what you've done with Sonny Cormac and those girls. It's no different than what I'm doing."

Everyone knows Sonny is bisexual. He practically broadcasts it to the world and flaunts it in his father's face to piss him off. But I didn't realize he was still carrying on with Aiden after all these years. Not with them living in different states and going to different colleges.

Sonny is at Harvard with us but two years behind. He's a Knight now and lives in the off-campus house with us.

"Shut up," Aiden snaps. "Don't fucking talk about him."

He looks upset, and I wonder what Sonny did to make Aiden so angry. They were friends back in high school. I didn't pay much attention to either of them. And with Sonny bringing home guys and girls to our house every weekend, I didn't think he was in a committed relationship with anyone.

"Then don't tell me what to do with my love life," Alex fires back at her twin. "I don't need your opinions, Aid."

"I don't need this shit." Cheeks flushed, Aiden gets up from the couch and walks down the hallway, disappearing into his bedroom.

"He acts like this any time I mention Sonny," she explains. "I don't know why."

"I do," Marcello admits.

He would know better than anyone since Sonny is Marcello's best friend.

"Tell me," Alex presses. "He gets so mad about Sonny."

"Not my story to tell, princess." Marcello shrugs. "Sorry, but you need to get that from your brother."

She pouts. "Everyone keeps secrets from me. I hate it."

Luca yanks Alex onto his lap, with her back pressed against his chest. His hand dips between her legs, and she whimpers. That's all it ever takes with her and Luca. He only has to breathe near Alex to get her panting and wanting more.

"Enough with the whining," he says against the shell of her ear, brushing his fingers on her inner thigh. "I meant what I said, Drea. It's time for you to toughen up. And if you're a good girl, I'll make sure you're more famous than my mother."

Her face lights up with a smile. "I'm not as talented as your mother was."

"Yes, you are."

It's the truth.

Alex is better than Evangeline. Some of her pieces are so powerful even I was breathless looking at them. And I don't have real feelings. So I know people who have them are blown away by her art.

Alex leans back and looks up at him. "You mean that?"

"I don't make a habit of saying things I don't mean." Luca squeezes her thigh. "When we're not here, I need you to remember what I said about being strong. We need a queen. No more crying or complaining when you don't see us. Do you understand me, baby girl?"

"Yes," she whispers, her eyes falling to the placement of Luca's hand that's about to skim over her pussy. She rocks her hips into his hand like a greedy little thing. He doesn't take the bait, so she looks at me, begging with her eyes to make her come.

I never deny her orgasms.

Neither does Bash.

But Luca will.

I hold up my hand and beckon her with my finger. "Come here, Pet."

"No." Luca's arm shoots out in front of her. "What did I tell you, Drea?"

"That guy almost killing me kinda interrupted something earlier," she says in a defiant tone. "I want Damian and Bash to finish what they started."

He raises an eyebrow, his gaze moving between us. "And what did they start?"

She bites her lip. "We were going to have sex."

Anger flashes across his face as he grabs her pussy. "This is ours, Drea. You better still be a virgin when we come for you again, or we're going to have a fucking problem."

Luca made a deal with Bash that he can have her virginity as long as he doesn't interfere with the marriage. But Alex doesn't know that. He wants her to behave until the time comes for us to claim her as a group.

She smacks his hand and wriggles out of his grasp. "You're so mean, Luca. I'm almost twenty-two and still haven't lost my virginity because you guys are saving it for some reason." Alex kneels on the couch between Luca and Bash. "Why won't any of you fuck me?"

The three of us look at Luca.

She watches our expressions and shakes her head, sliding off the couch to get away from Luca. "Of course it's because of you. Why am I not surprised? I know you wouldn't let your brothers see or talk to me all through college. Why are you so jealous of them?"

He rolls his eyes. "I'm not."

"Could have fooled me," she shouts, cheeks flushed with anger. "Every time Damian and Bastian touched me in high school, you looked like you were going to explode."

Luca doesn't like being challenging and hops up from the couch, effortlessly tossing Alex over his shoulder. "You wanna talk back, baby? Let's see how good you take my cock." He slaps her ass. "Are you ready for that? I'll treat you like a slut. Think you can handle me?"

Luca will probably split her tight cunt in half. He's a lot bigger than Bash and me. At least three inches longer and a lot thicker. Even I wouldn't want to get fucked with a cock that big. Bash is just right, the perfect nine inches.

Either Bash or Marcello needs to take Alex's virginity.

They will be sweet and go slow. Not Luca or me. I lose control when I have sex and can't guarantee I won't hurt her. And Luca is just as much of an animal as me. She'll probably need stitches if he gets to her first.

Luca lowers Alex onto the dining room table so she's on her stomach, ass sticking up. He peels down her yoga pants and panties and runs his palm over her pale skin. "You wanna fuck, baby? I'm not nice. I'll tear up your pussy, bruise your pretty body, and make a fucking mess." He whacks her ass, leaving a red handprint. "Is this how you want to lose your virginity?"

"No," she whimpers. "Not like this."

He pulls her panties and pants back up and flips her onto her ass. "Keep your legs shut and stop offering yourself to my brothers." His hand palms her pussy. "I better see blood on my dick the first time I fuck you."

Luca won't back out of the deal with Bastian, not when the marriage is more important to him. He's only saying this to make a point that her pussy belongs to us.

Alex's teeth graze her bottom lip. "Okay."

Luca lifts her off the table and sets her feet on the ground. "Shower and get ready for bed. We're leaving soon. You better be in that bed before I walk out the door."

Bash pushes himself up from the couch, and I follow him over to Alex.

He extends his hand to her. "C'mon, Cherry. I'll help you wash your pussy."

She giggles. "You're so dirty, Bash." Then she looks at me. "Are you coming?"

Of course, I am.

I nod, giving her a creepy grin I can't contain. "You should know by now you don't get one of us without the other."

152

Chapter Twenty-Three

Two years later...

I HAVE WAITED YEARS TO CLAIM *HER*. YEARS OF THINKING about how my life will change once she's *ours*.

"It's time to bring our queen home." Luca unlocks Alex's front door of the apartment she shares with her twin brother —because of course we have a key—and he pushes it open, entering the living room. "And she's not going to like it."

I shut the door behind me and take in the small space. Alex and Aiden are the heirs to Wellington Pharmaceuticals, and yet they haven't spent a cent of their trust funds. They live in a shitty—by my standards—apartment in a crowded section of Brooklyn called Williamsburg.

The headquarters of both Salvatore Global and Atlantic Airlines is right over the bridge in Manhattan. Luca is the CEO of his company, while Bastian serves as the leader of our airline. He's better at communicating with people than me. I prefer to deal with people only when it's absolutely necessary.

Bash moves beside Luca, grinning like the Joker. "Her cherry is still mine, brother."

I could give a damn about taking her virginity. As long as Bash fucks her first and lets me lick the blood from her pussy, I'm good.

I like blood.

How it smells.

How it tastes.

Feels on my fingers.

My tongue.

My cock.

She's going to bleed for one of us, and when she does, we'll all get to savor the moment. Our girl isn't getting one of us without the other.

"If you knock her up," Luca snaps at Bastian. "I'll cut off your dick and jam it down your throat."

Bash tips his head back and laughs. "She's worth it."

Luca rolls his eyes. "I don't share your obsession with her. And if you think for one second she wants any of us after not talking to her for two years, you've got another thing coming."

"Yeah, you do." Aiden walks into the living room with paint all over him. "Stay the fuck away from my sister. And get the fuck out of my house."

He's covered from the neck down in black tattoos, wearing dark blue jeans and a tight gray shirt stained with red and black paint. His hair is blond and curly like his twin's, but he keeps it short on the top to tame the curls, unlike Alex, whose hair is always wild and looks like she's just been fucked.

Aiden clutches a paintbrush between his long fingers like it's a weapon. Fucking idiot should know all of us are carrying guns. Not like I need one, anyway.

My hands are weapons.

Aiden pockets the paintbrush and removes his cell phone from his jeans. His fingers fly across the keypad, and I hear the unmistakable sound of a text message sent on his iPhone. He must be warning Alex that we're here. They have waited for this day for years, not knowing when we would come to collect our prize.

"Is that any way to greet your future brother-in-law?" Luca says in a mocking tone as he approaches him. He snaps his fingers at Bash. "Get the rope."

"What?" Aiden inches backward, shaking his head. "You four are fucking crazy."

"I prefer psychotic," I tell him, removing the hunting knife from the sheath attached to my belt. Running the blade over my palm, I step closer. "Now, we can do this the easy way or the hard way. Your choice, Wellington."

"Fuck you."

Aiden is smart and darts down the hallway, forcing me to follow him. Bastian is beside me with a red rope in his hand. The same rope he's used to tie me to his bed.

I glance over at him, thinking of all the ways Alex gets both of us what we want. He wants normalcy, a woman who can balance out the two of us.

And I want him.

Well, I want her, too.

But I want him *more*.

"Let me handle him." Bastian taps my shoulder and enters the dining room. He snaps the rope in both hands, a sly grin aimed at Aiden. "Unless you plan to jump out the window, Wellington, you better submit. It will hurt less."

Bash got into bondage after he saw experts do it at The Mansion. I was sixteen when I got my first kill, and after we crossed the line, he wanted to punish himself. He thought bondage would allow him to do that. But instead of punishing himself, he did it to women.

And me.

He can choke me, gag me, do anything he wants as long as we both get to come.

"I'm not going back to Devil's Creek with you." Aiden reaches into the server beside the dining room table and pulls out a butter knife. "And neither is Alex."

Bastian laughs. "What do you plan to do with that?" He shakes his head. "Don't be stupid. This doesn't have to hurt."

"Fuck you," Aiden hisses. "Do whatever you want to me.

My sister will never be yours. I don't care what deal our grandfather made with your dad."

"Hurry up." Luca snaps his fingers at Bastian like he's a dog. "We don't have all day."

Without arguing with Luca, Bastian bares his teeth to show his anger. But he doesn't say anything. We never correct Luca in front of outsiders. We work as a team and never reveal any weaknesses. Our father says that we must present a unified front at all times. If not, others will see it as a weakness and try to take our power.

Bastian inches toward Aiden with me at his side. Between the two of us, we'll have his ass tied to a dining chair in under a minute. So I grab one arm while Bastian takes the other.

"Get the fuck off me!" Aiden isn't as bulky as Marcello, but he's thick in the arms and tries to fight us. "I'm not going with you. I don't care what my grandfather says."

He lands a punch to my shoulder and one to Bash's arm. We ignore it and advance on him, flipping him onto the table on his stomach. A groan escapes his throat.

Pressing Aiden's cheek to the table, I hold him down and pin one arm behind his back. Bash takes the other and works quickly to secure the rope in place before we push Aiden into a chair. I help Bash tie the last knot to the wooden chair, giving him a proud smile.

He winks.

"Let's go," Luca says to the three of us, his blue eyes gleaming with mischief.

He's always plotting something, and on a day like this, it's got something to do with our girl.

"You can't fucking leave me here," Aiden snaps, his tanned skin red from struggling so hard against the restraints.

"Yes, we can," Luca fires back. "And we will let you rot until you choose to accept your place with The Devil's Knights."

"Never." Aiden rocks the chair to each side, doing his best

to tip it over in the hopes the wood will snap. "I want no part of your fucked up secret society."

"Too bad." Luca clicks his tongue. "You're going to be a Knight. It's your birthright."

"Nah." Aiden shakes his head, spit dripping from his lip. "Fuck that. I never wanted to be a Wellington. I wasn't born into this shit, and I want nothing to do with it."

Before Alex and Aiden moved to Devil's Creek, their last name was Fox. They were so far removed from our world they didn't even know it existed. But he's had six years to get used to his future.

"Your sister will be our queen," Luca reminds him, producing a bandana from his pocket. "Whether you like it or not. And you will bow at her fucking feet when I crown her. So get your fucking shit together because you have one week." He pulls the banana over Aiden's mouth and ties it behind his head to keep him quiet. "If you're not in Devil's Creek by then, I will send the Knights after you. And you don't want that."

The Devil's Knights have never had a queen before. Knights swear an oath to protect each other at all costs. And once Alex becomes our queen, every Knight will be bound to her in a ceremony we call *Legare*.

Luca glances down at his cell phone and snaps his fingers at us. "She's here."

Of course, he knows. Luca has been keeping tabs on Alex for years.

Every text.

Every call.

Every email.

He has all of her chat and Internet search history. We know every dirty secret and all of her desires. There's nothing we don't know about Alexandrea Wellington.

I waited too long to claim my Pet, and as Alex enters the

apartment, my heart beats faster. My pulse pounds in my ears. The blood turns to fire in my veins.

Whenever she's near, I get the same feeling as a kill. My blood pumps faster, rushing to my cock.

We stand in the living room, dressed in black Brioni suits. The four of us line up to block her path. She'll go straight to Aiden once she realizes he's not coming to save her.

Not happening.

Alex's pretty, pink lips part, her eyes moving to each of us. And when they land on me, I lick my lips. My expression says, *Hello, Pet. I've missed you.*

Chapter Twenty-Four

I'VE HUNTED ENOUGH PEOPLE TO KNOW WHEN THEY'VE GIVEN up. And as I stare at Alex, I know she's ready for a fight. She isn't going to submit to us, not without us breaking her first.

Our girl wants us.

Needs us.

Literally, she needs our protection from her family's enemies. She doesn't know about all the death threats and men who have tried to harm her. She's the heir to billions and has a target on her back.

I have killed over twenty men in the past three years.

For her.

And I would do it again.

There's no line I wouldn't cross for Alex. No obstacle too high to keep my girl safe. She's going to be mine and Bastian's someday.

Just the three of us.

Once Luca gets his heir.

Bastian steps toward her with a wicked smirk tugging at the right corner of his mouth. He clutches her cheek, staring at her beautiful face. "I've been waiting for you, Cherry. Did you miss me?"

"No, get your hands off me." She shoves his hand away from her face, baring her teeth like a trapped animal ready to tear into his flesh. "I'm not your Cherry. You lost the privilege of calling me that years ago." Alex tries to move around us, but we're in her way, so she yells, "Aiden."

He's not coming.

I laugh.

So does Luca.

Bastian scratches his jaw, studying her face like she's a puzzle he wants to solve. As usual, Marcello says nothing. He stares at her, lost in his thoughts. While he's never outright said he wants Alex, I know he does. I've caught him jerking off to the surveillance footage of her more than once over the years.

Hell, I have, too.

And so has Bash.

I've even gone as far as having deep fake porn made of Alex. Bondage. Whipping. Rough shit that would make the real Alex's head spin.

The girls in the videos have the same body type as Alex—lots of curves and big tits. But the footage is digitally altered so the girls have Alex's face. I gave one of the videos to Bash for his twenty-fourth birthday. He loved it so much that he sucked my cock twice that night.

Alex throws her hands on her narrow hips. She's put on weight over the years, and I like the changes in her body. I can't wait to grab her big ass and spread those thick thighs while I shove my tongue between her wet folds. I miss touching her, teasing her.

"What the fuck are you assholes doing in my apartment?" Alex asks, lip quivering in anger. "And where the fuck is my brother?"

"Your brother is safe." Bastian smirks. "For now."

Furious, she slams her palms into his chest and attempts to get past him.

But I grab her wrist.

Dipping my head down, my lips inches from her earlobe, I say, "Haven't you learned your lesson, Pet?"

She knows better than to challenge us.

We always win.

Alex laughs in my face. "I'm not your pet, you sick fuck."

I curl my fingers around her throat, forcing my Pet to submit to her master. "You're whatever I want you to be, Pet. Get out of line this time, and your brother will pay the price."

Her long fingernails dig into my forearm, but I embrace the pain and refuse to loosen my grip on her.

"Let me go, psycho."

"Now, now, Pet." I stroke the side of her face, smirking. "It's not nice to call your owner names. You know why we're here. Now be a good girl and go pack your shit."

"It's time to choose, Drea."

Only Luca calls her that. He's never admitted to us why he does. Just told us to fuck off when we asked him.

Why would he give the woman he hates a nickname? It's so out of character for my brother. And yet, he did.

Luca moves beside me, glaring at Alex with pure hatred. "We let you off your leash long enough. You're coming with us to Devil's Creek."

I hold her tighter, my breath warming her cheek. "This time, we're keeping you."

She gasps. "I'm not yours to keep."

"When you sign a contract with the devil," Bastian says, shoving his fingers roughly through her hair, "your soul belongs to him."

She raises her hand to slap him, but he catches her arm in midair.

"Don't test me, Cherry. I'll bend you over my knee and spank your ass until it's black and blue."

Full of fire and spite, she rolls her eyes. "Your threats don't scare me."

I'm turned on by her anger and want to pin her to the floor and fuck her senseless. If not for the deal I made with my brothers, I would. But Luca made us agree not to fuck her. We have to do it together or not at all.

Alex walks away like she doesn't have to listen to us. She's been ours since we were eighteen. I don't know why she tries to deny it. Sure, she's pissed about us letting her live her life in peace for the past two years. Without us around, she was safer.

I'm annoyed with Alex's attitude, so I lift her in my arms, throwing her onto the living room couch. "I see you're going to be a pain in my ass, Pet."

I shove her face into the cushion and hold her down while I yank the skirt up her thighs. I'm surprised to see our girl is wearing a thong. She didn't wear them back in high school. Only when I ripped off her panties and gave her new ones.

I snap the string so it slaps her skin. "Such a dirty little whore. This skirt barely covers your ass."

Bastian sits on the cushion beside her head, running his fingers through her curls. "We're not sharing you with the world, Cherry." He slides his hand down her back and over her ass, grabbing her cheek. "This is ours. And you better remember that the next time you leave the house dressed like a slut."

"I'm not dressed like a slut. Fuck you."

Bastian looks at me with a wild expression on his face. "You want to go first?"

Alex wiggles beneath us, kicking her legs, but it only encourages me to press down on her with my weight. I bend down and bite her earlobe. "Time to take your punishment."

"Punishment for what?"

"For talking back," I say as my palm crashes down on her backside.

She's taken plenty of our punishments before. And no matter how many times she pretends to hate it, she's always wet for us. Always begging us for more.

I missed this.

Missed *her*.

My pretty little Pet is about to be mine in a more permanent way. She's ours to share and break. And despite her attitude, she wants this, too. Alex satiates a sick need inside me.

Luca and Marcello watch as I dole out her punishment. I give her exactly three whacks before I switch places with Bastian. He spanks her three times before reaching between her legs to test her wetness.

Our girl is dripping for us, her cum dampening the fabric. Bastian flashes a slick grin at me. He's satisfied with the result, and so am I. Every time we touch her, she's wet for us.

Luca never touches.

He only watches.

So does Marcello.

But they want her.

We all do.

"Always so wet for men you hate," Bastian teases with the click of his tongue. "Did you save yourself for me, Cherry?"

"She's not yours, Bash," Luca growls.

Bastian glances at him. "Right, she's *ours.*"

He helps Alex to her feet, and she's so embarrassed by how we make her feel that her cheeks flush.

She leaves the living room and heads toward her brother. "Aiden, where are you?"

Luca tips his head, and we go after her, keeping our distance as she enters the dining room. She gasps when she finds her brother tied to a wooden dining chair with his hands behind his back and a bandana covering his mouth.

Alex moves behind the chair, tugging on the knots, but it's useless. She knows Bastian tied them and won't get past the first one.

Her eyes find Bash. "Untie him."

He stuffs his hands into his pockets and smirks. "Say the magic words, Cherry."

I see the look of defeat cross over her face. She knows

what Bastian wants from her. It's the only thing he's wanted for years.

Her cherry.

"I'm yours," she whispers.

A sly grin tugs at his mouth as he approaches her. "I didn't hear you, Cherry. Say it again."

Lips pressed together, she glances at Aiden, knowing she has no choice. Aiden shakes his head, screaming for her to stop but the bandana muffles his voice.

Alex wets her lips and sighs. "I'm yours, Bash."

He clutches her hips. "Answer my question from earlier."

"I'm still a virgin."

We made sure none of the dumb fucks at her college touched her. Any man who got too close was suddenly too busy. Maybe they were even dead if I felt extra stabby that night. It all depended on how much they tried to pursue her. Alex is a twenty-four-year-old virgin because we want all of her firsts.

"Good girl." Bastian rubs his thumb across her lips. "It's time to take you home."

Chapter Twenty-Five

I THOUGHT SHE WOULD PUT UP MORE OF A FIGHT. IT disappoints me that my Pet came willingly. She didn't speak a word after fighting with Luca about her fate. He only had to put his hands on her, and she was melting into his arms.

Luca has a strange hold over Alex. They do this dance where they pretend to hate each other. But if the past is any indicator of the present, she still gets wet every time he gives her any attention.

She's starved for him, mostly because he's the only one who doesn't show her interest. His anger and rage over her mother killing his hasn't quelled over the years. And once he does touch her, he's going to unleash his fury, making her wish she stayed away from him.

As the limo pulls up in front of a black jet that reads *Salvatore Global* on the side in red lettering, Alex sighs. She knows there's no escaping fate. Her place is among us as the future Queen of The Devil's Knights.

She belongs with *us*.

Alex sits between Bash and me at the table with Luca across from us. He glares at her, but I can see the desire written all over his face. Luca usually wears an emotionless mask. I get it because I do, too. But we've been brothers long enough to read the few emotions he does have.

Alex's hands tremble, and to still her nerves, she clasps her hands together. Bastian notices and moves his hand to her thigh, clutching her bare skin with possession.

She doesn't fight him.

Like she should.

Instead, she does the worst thing possible and ignores him, staring out the window as the plane lifts off from the ground.

Bash looks at me, a sick smile plastered on his lips. I know what he's thinking when he inches his hand up her thigh. He wants her to say no, to tell him to stop him. She rarely does and gives him nothing.

He shoves the skirt up her thighs, so I can see her thong. His fingers graze over the thin fabric, and I can see by her heart beating faster as he touches her. I watch them, tapping my ring on the wooden table. It's platinum with onyx chips that form a snake into the Salvatore crest. All of my brothers and father have one.

I have to do something to occupy my hand, so I keep tapping until she's looking at me.

"I'm living at Wellington Manor," Alex says like she has a choice.

Luca smirks.

I tap my ring on the table again. She jumps at the sound, keeping her focus on Luca. A beat passes in silence. Marcello is lounging on the couch across from us, typing on his phone. He doesn't pay us any mind as usual.

Alex looks to each of us for a response. We don't give her one, drowning her fear with silence.

Bastian brushes his fingers up and down her thighs and cuts the tension in the air by saying, "Sick of us already, Cherry? The fun hasn't even begun."

"You don't have a choice." Luca hasn't spoken much, but his eyes haven't left her. "Our estate is your new and permanent home."

Bastian lifts Alex's leg on top of his, and I'm jealous of

how easily he touches her without overthinking it. What we do will never see the light, all by design.

"We own you now," Bastian tells her, gripping her inner thigh. "You're ours to do with as we please."

Alex snorts with laughter, still feisty and ready to fight, even though she's trapped with us. "Keep telling yourself that, Bash. I hope you like fucking corpses because I won't enjoy a single second of you on top of me. In fact, why don't we go into the bedroom and get this over with, so I can go home?"

I shove up the sleeves of my suit jacket and rest my tattooed forearms on the table, searing her skin with my eyes. Considering her request, I look at Bastian, wondering how he will respond. Because if he drags her into the bedroom, I'm going with them.

He lowers his head so their lips almost touch. "You make my cock so fucking hard, Cherry."

She licks her lips while staring at his. Bash gave Alex her first kiss, and I can tell she's thinking about it. And so am I. Because I was jealous that she got to kiss him when I had been waiting years for him to lower his guard.

Her eyes graze over his lips before moving up to his gray eyes. "Let's get something straight. You don't scare me. I don't care if I have to fuck all of you. Threaten me all you want. I hate you. All of you. You're fucking deviants."

I shrug, unaffected by her feelings for us, and laugh. Like we care if she hates us. It's all bullshit, anyway. Her words say one thing, but how her body responds to us says another.

Luca drains the scotch from his glass, eying her up like a predator. "We all have to be something. Might as well be someone everyone fears."

Alex scoffs. "I don't fear any of you. I despise you. There's a difference."

"You came with us too easily." Luca's voice is devoid of any emotion. "As Bash said, you didn't even fight us."

Amused, he shakes his head. "At the very least, you could have screamed or begged. You handed over your virgin pussy to the men you pretend to hate." A smirk tugs at the corner of his mouth. "Now, the real question remains. Which one of us will claim you first?"

Chapter Twenty-Six

She's ours to claim.

The thought rolls around in my sick mind as Bastian sits beside me on the bed. We're in his bedroom at the Salvatore Estate, waiting for Marcello to help Alex settle into her new bedroom.

Her new life.

I put my hand on Bash's thigh, and his head snaps to me. "We need to break her in. Teach her what *we* like."

His eyes move to my lips, and I lick them to see how he will respond. Mirroring me, he tugs his bottom lip into his mouth, and I consider taking it between my teeth. My skin ignites from the flames spreading up my arms and down my thighs.

"You've been patient with me, D." His hand covers mine. "But I don't know how this is going to work."

"Bash, stop overthinking everything."

Last night, he had my dick jammed down his throat, swallowing my cum. We were watching one of the deep fake porn videos of Alex. She will probably kill us when she sees them. But whatever, she can watch them with us while we fuck her.

Bastian needs her to make what we're doing okay. It's been eight years of us fucking around and fighting about his feelings for me. He'll never leave me, nor me him. Letting go of Bash would be like ripping my soul in half. And he can't walk away from me either.

Our fates are intertwined.

I adjust my cock, and Bastian glances down, his chest rising and falling with each breath. He's also hard, his length tenting his dress pants.

He's excited she's finally here. It's time for him to let go of his fear and unleash his desires. We made a deal that if she's okay with us, we will find a way to make this work.

Just the three of us.

Despite what Alex thinks, we're not complete fucking assholes. She's not stuck with us. However, she is not getting away from Luca. He'll force her to choose him and drag her screaming down the aisle if that's what it takes to get an heir with Founders' blood.

He *needs* this marriage.

I unzip his pants, and he leans back on the bed, propping himself up with his elbows. We need this before we go into her bedroom and test the water. The deal we made with Luca forces us to behave. We can play with her, but we can't fuck her.

I whip out Bastian's big dick and give it a few strokes. He's thick and grows in my hand, precum sliding down his shaft and onto my hand. I bend down and lick the tip, lapping up his cum.

Bash groans and tugs at the ends of my short hair. "Fuck, D." He hisses. "Suck my dick." Pushing on my head, he rocks his hips, and I open my mouth wider to deep-throat him. "Oh, fuck. Goddamn. That feels... Fuck." His eyes close halfway, but he's still looking down at me, watching his cock slide in and out of my mouth. "Why are you so good at this?"

He says that I give him the best head he's ever gotten. Not even the pros at The Mansion suck his dick like I do. And no one will ever compare to me. I know what he wants and give it to him every time. No one will ever be as in tune with his body as I am.

His cum shoots into the back of my throat, and I suck him

off until I get the last drop. Then, I sit up and lick my lips, savoring his cum.

"Things are going to be different," he says, trying to catch his breath. "Now that she's here… We can be ourselves."

"Yeah?"

He nods.

"But you gotta get out of your head first, Bash."

"I'm trying." He unzips my pants, fisting my shaft hard since he knows what I like. "God, I love your dick." His eyes lower, and he licks his lips. "It's fucking perfect."

"We're each other's only and longest relationship," I tell him. "It was always going to be the two of us. You know that, right?"

He stops jerking my shaft but still keeps his hand on me. Our eyes meet, and there's a palpable energy in the air. "There's never been anyone else. Just you and Alex." His hand glides up and down my skin, and when he rubs his thumb over the tip, I groan. "We gotta make this work. She's right for us."

"But she needs to choose Luca," I grunt as he jerks harder.

"She will," he says, convinced. "The four of us can share her. Luca says he doesn't want her when he does. And you've seen how Marcello watches over her. So there's no way he's letting her walk away."

We never gave a damn about the marriage. Our brothers can have that. It's nothing more than a piece of paper, anyway.

Bastian ends our conversation by sucking my dick into his mouth, swirling his tongue over the tip to tease me. He cups my balls with one hand while jerking my shaft with the other. A few times, he even uses his teeth because he knows how much I like the pain.

If a woman did that, I would probably kill her. But when Bash does it, I can't get enough.

"Harder." I grab him by the neck and force more of me

down his throat, getting even more teeth on the way up. He does it on purpose, and I love it. "Fuck, Bash."

My legs tremble as he jerks my cock faster. Seconds later, I come into his mouth. And like a good boy, he sits up and lets me see the cum on his tongue.

I wrap my hand around his throat and lean forward, testing him to see if he will push me away. When he doesn't, I stick out my tongue and taste myself on his lips. I lick the seam of his mouth without taking it further.

Just a few licks.

He swallows my cum and pulls away. "You're sick, you know that?"

I laugh. "And you're just now realizing that?"

I've been making him show me my cum on his tongue since we were teenagers. It's the only power I have over him. When he's caught up in the moment, he does whatever I ask as long as he gets to come.

"You may scare Alex away with your cum fetish." Bastian rises from the bed, tucks his dick back into his boxers, and zips his pants. "Maybe tone down your usual until she gets used to us."

I fix my pants and stand beside him. "If she thinks that's bad, wait until she finds out about my blood fetish."

He shakes his head, grinning. "That girl has no idea what she signed up for. We're all fucking sick in our own ways." His hands touch my chest, and my heart beats faster with his closeness. "I love you, D. And I love her, too. The three of us are going to be happy. I know it."

I smile, which only happens when I'm around Bash. "I never thought either of us would get to be happy." I shake my head in disbelief. "People like me don't deserve it."

Bastian inches his hands up my chest until his arms are hooked around my neck. "We deserve it after all the shit we've been through. I know you don't always believe that because of the bad things you've done. But it's you and me. Always. And now we have Alex."

They.

Are.

Mine.

Want more of my books?

Join The Frost Society, where I post chapters of my books as I write them, including more books set in the Devil's Creek world.

You can also get access to my serials and novels library, download my eBooks in advance of the releases, read bonus content about your favorite characters, get signed paperbacks and swag, and other bookish things.

Get all of the bookish perks at JillianFrost.com.

.

Also by Jillian Frost

Princes of Devil's Creek

Cruel Princes

Vicious Queen

Savage Knights

Battle King

Boardwalk Mafia

Boardwalk Kings

Boardwalk Queen

Boardwalk Reign

Devil's Creek Standalones

The Darkest Prince

Wicked Union

For a complete list of books, visit JillianFrost.com.

About the Author

Jillian Frost is a dark romance author who believes even the villain deserves a happily ever after. When she's not plotting all the ways to disrupt the lives of her characters, you can usually find Jillian by the pool, soaking up the Florida sunshine.

Learn more about Jillian's books at JillianFrost.com

Made in the USA
Columbia, SC
31 May 2024

36456500R00117